SCRATCH FEVER

Books *by* Max Allan Collins

Nolan Novels

FLY PAPER

HARD CASH

SCRATCH FEVER

HUSH MONEY

MOURN THE LIVING

SPREE

Quarry Novels

QUARRY

QUARRY'S LIST

QUARRY'S DEAL

QUARRY'S CUT

QUARRY'S VOTE

from PERFECT CRIME BOOKS

SCRATCH FEVER

MAX ALLAN COLLINS

With an Introduction by the Author

PERFECT CRIME BOOKS

Printed in the United States of America.

Perfect Crime Books™ is a registered Trademark.

Cover by Christopher Mills.

This book is a work of fiction. The characters and institutions are products of the Author's imagination and do not refer to actual persons or institutions.

Library of Congress Cataloging-in-Publication Data
Collins, Max Allan
Scratch Fever/Max Allan Collins

ISBN: 978-1-935797-26-5

Perfect Crime Books Edition: May 2012

Introduction

SCRATCH FEVER holds a somewhat unique position in my Nolan series. The first five novels were written in the late sixties through the mid-'70s. But only the first two, *Bait Money* and *Blood Money*, were published in the seventies (both in 1973). The others, because of a merger between publishers Curtis Books and Popular Library, went into that terrible limbo called inventory. Promises of publication were made but not kept. And around 1980, I got the rights back.

With astonishing speed, Pinnacle Books picked up the five books (three of which had never seen publication, remember). I did some rewriting and updating, and suddenly Nolan was again back in business. But Pinnacle was something of a relentless publisher when it came to crime–they offered me a *six-*book contract.

Which meant that, after seven or eight years or so, I would be returning to the series, with the express instructions that the jump from '70s book to '80s book be seamless.

I think it is. Probably this is my favorite of that first batch of Nolan novels (even if it is, sort of, a one-book "second batch"). I was really getting the hang of writing low-life villains who retained a recognizable humanity, and both Nolan and Jon were getting nice and round, which in particular for Nolan, a genre type if ever there was one, was a good trick. But in *Scratch Fever*, you meet a Nolan with a genuine relationship going on with his girl Sherry (and to him she is a "girl"), not to mention real concern for his partner-in-crime, Jon. You also will find out what happens when somebody fucks with Nolan's dog, and I don't mean the terrier next door.

Two things particularly please me about this novel.

The character Julie, returned from *Hard Cash*, is a particularly good femme fatale, I think. I can say this looking back at the novel since I hardly remember writing the thing, and can take it on its own terms. (I do remember that the two hitmen in this novel were inspired by an apparently gay pair of killers in the classic Joseph H. Lewis film, *The Big Combo*. If you are a real buff, you'll realize that this pits Lee Van Cleef against . . . Lee Van Cleef.)

The other thing is the presence of rock music in the plot or anyway the ambience. I have played in rock bands since high school, starting around 1966. There have been occasional stretches where I haven't been out there playing, but mostly I have, right up to the present. (The next place my band Crusin' is appearing at is called "Ducky's Lagoon.")

The Barn, the venue where Jon and his band the Nodes are appearing, is based on a now-defunct joint called the Pub, where Crusin' played every other weekend for at least two years. This is a very accurate rendition of that club. When I wrote the novel, I had just quit the band, who went on without me as a trio playing New Wave under the name the Ones. I returned before long, but in some sense, writing about Jon as a rock musician and this particular venue was a kind of valedictory. Premature as it turns out, but nonetheless *Scratch Fever* marks the most major convergence between my two worlds–writing crime novels and playing rock music–and, for that reason if no other, it holds a special place in my hardboiled heart.

All of my early novels–virtually everything that Perfect Crime has reprinted–were written when I was a working rock musician. For several years, playing rock was my major source of income . . . particularly the fallow writing period between when I wrote the Nolan, Mallory and Quarry novels, and landed the Dick Tracy comic strip. Pinnacle publishing Nolan would follow soon, and Mallory finally seeing print at Walker, and Nathan Heller coming to life at St. Martin's Press and changing my career.

Somewhat ironically, *Scratch Fever* is the first book of that second, much more successful time . . . so it's no wonder it's my favorite of the first seven Nolan novels.

I hope you like it, too.

MAX ALLAN COLLINS
January 2012

1

1

JON, ON STAGE, sweating, singing, mouth against the wire mesh ball of the microphone, hands on the black keys of the keyboard, looked out across the underlit, crowded dance floor, smoke drifting like fog, and saw somebody who was supposed to be dead.

He blinked the sweat away and looked again.

She was gone.

But he had seen her. Recognized her. He shouldn't have been able to—her hair was different, still long, brushing her shoulders, but streaked blonde now, heavily so—and she wore tinted glasses with dark frames. He'd never seen her in glasses before, but she had the kind of face that a change of hair and the addition of glasses made no less distinctive.

It was mostly her mouth, he supposed: full lips that wore a

faint, permanent pout, like Elke Sommer, but cruel, somehow. Smug. A feature that attracted and repelled, promised and threatened. As did that shape of hers—big boobs, tiny waist, wide hips, perfect ass. She was a sexual exaggeration, a Vargas girl come to life. She was Julie.

Julie, in white skirt and jacket and black cardigan, looking like a businesswoman, coldly chic, talking to Bob, the club manager, a six-four former farmer who was sitting with her over at the bar, stage right, handing her a drink.

Only that had been before Jon blinked.

Now Bob was sitting next to an empty stool, looking toward the back of the room, the drink in his hand extended toward nobody.

Shit, Jon thought; she saw *me*, too, recognized me. He felt a chill, despite the heat of the stage lights, the row of alternating red/blue/yellow spots strung on a pole above him, the system the band carried with them.

No. She wouldn't have recognized him; she wouldn't expect to see him playing on stage with a rock band. She wouldn't know him with his hair cut off. He was just another musician, short, muscular, curly haired; there were hundreds of people who looked like him.

Yeah. Sure.

The song was over, he suddenly realized ("Pump It Up," by Elvis Costello), and he should be introducing the next one, but he couldn't remember what it was. He glanced over at the list of songs taped to the monitor speaker next to his portable organ (an old Vox Super Continental double keyboard), but the salty sweat in his eyes kept him from being able to focus on it.

The rest of the band, Les, Roc, Mick, Toni, stood and looked at him, waiting, and there was one of those two- or three-second pauses that most audiences don't notice but seem an eternity to the people on stage, and then his eyes focused and he saw on the typed song list "Accidents Never Happen" just below "Pump It Up."

"We'd like to do one by Blondie," he heard himself saying, his

voice echoing across the hall, *"featuring Toni. She isn't blonde, but she's more fun."*

Toni did a little Debbie Harry salute/smile at the audience, and the faces out there smiled back at her, accompanied by a few laughs, and they went into the song.

The band—which was called the Nodes—did a lot of Blondie material, because Toni did resemble Blondie's Debbie Harry just a little, though her hair was brunette (but then again so was Debbie Harry's, really), and she had a similar busty little figure and could mimic Ms. Harry's voice to perfection, as well as half a dozen other women's, from Ronnie Spector to Pat Benatar to Lene Lovich, which was no small feat. Toni was the most popular member of the band, and Jon didn't mind. But Les, Roc, and Mick did, and that was probably the major reason this was the band's last gig.

After seven very successful months—they'd been playing the Wisconsin/Iowa/Illinois club circuit and pulling down $1500 a week, which for a band without a hit record was good money—the Nodes were going their separate ways. Or at least Les, Roc, and Mick were going one way, staying together as a trio, while Jon and Toni went another, to a tryout in St Paul, next week, with a new band. Girl singers and keyboard players were always in demand.

Besides, there was a split in musical tastes among the band. Jon and Toni both liked new wave rock, like the Elvis Costello and Blondie numbers that dominated the song list; but the rest of the band (who had been together for years under various names, among them Eargasm, Fried Smoke and Deep Pink) were into heavy-metal rock, and it was at their insistence that material like Aerosmith and Ted Nugent stayed on the list, much to Jon and Toni's distaste.

The club they were playing was called the Barn, and it was in the country, between two cornfields, ten miles outside Burlington, Iowa. Part of it actually was a barn, or had been before it was turned into a restaurant, with the rough wood and red and white checkered tablecloths and barbecued ribs you'd expect of a restaurant that used to be a barn. A huge tin shed had been erected next to the restaurant and in this, still in a rustic manner, an Old Town setting had been created, with fake storefronts lining either side of a big dance floor. Between storefronts and dance floor were more tables with red and white checked cloths, and there was a bar on either side, plus another in back, in the area that connected the restaurant and the club.

The audience here was a young one, teens to late twenties, with enough people in their thirties to make it a difficult mix for a band to please. The drinking age was twenty-one, but fake I.D.s were more common than real ones in clubs like this one. The manager, Bob Hale, insisted that the bands he booked in play "nostalgia," which meant fifties and sixties rock, and the Nodes carried plenty of songs in that area. And the band dressed like a British sixties group: sportcoats and skinny ties and short hair. Even Toni had a Beatle haircut and wore a skinny tie with her white shirt—of course, the white shirt and tie were all Toni wore, that and pantyhose, the shirt hitting her mid-thigh, like a mini-skirt, which was Jon's idea of "nostalgia."

Jon knew that to exist as a band in the Midwest it was necessary to cater to slightly crazed club owners, like Bob, who wanted bands that could appeal to everybody. The Nodes' tongue-in-cheek clean-cut look helped accomplish that, and the songs by the Stones, Kinks and Beatles, plus sixties camp like "96 Tears," "Dirty Water," and "Woolly Bully," pleased the patrons in their thirties as well as the eighteen-year-olds.

At the end of "Accidents Never Happen," tall, skinny lead guitarist Roc went into "Cat Scratch Fever." Several male voices, out in the smoky crowd, yelped and hooted. It was a popular song. It was also Jon and Toni's cue to step offstage for a break; neither her vocals nor his keyboards were required on that opus, and besides, they hated it.

There was a little room off to stage right, behind one of the fake storefronts, where he and Toni went to wait out the song.

He could hear Roc's toneless voice echoing out there: *"Make her pussy purr. . . ."*

4

"Why do they like that shit?" Jon asked.

Toni was sitting on one of the hard black flight cases a guitar amp was carried in; her short, nice legs were crossed as she unscrewed the cap of a bottle of Cutty Sark.

"You mean Les and Roc and Mick," she asked, "or the crowd?"

"Both."

"Beats the fuck out of me," she said, and took a swig of the whiskey; her little-girl face lit up as it rolled down her throat "Then again, this is Iowa," she added.

Out in the other room, Roc's guitar whined; people whooped.

"If Iowa sucks so bad," he said, "why'd you leave New Jersey?"

It was a question he'd asked many times these past months.

The answer he got he'd heard before: "1 thought maybe I'd stand out in a cornfield."

He usually laughed at that, but this time he didn't. He was thinking about the woman he'd seen—in the white skirt and black sweater. He was thinking about Julie.

"Something on your mind, Jonny?"

"I don't know. Maybe."

"Cat scratch fever . . ."

"I thought you looked like something threw you on stage there for a second—couple songs ago. Something to that?"

"Maybe."

She smiled; she really looked like Debbie Harry when she smiled. "Bet you spotted somebody in the crowd. An old girlfriend. Am I right, Jonny?"

"Not exactly."

"Well, these are your old stomping grounds, aren't they?"

"Cat scratch fever . . . Cat scratch fever . . ."

"Not really. I'm eighty or a hundred miles from home."

Home was Iowa City. Or it used to be, before he and Toni had met in a music store; she'd been playing with Dagwood, a group that did nothing but Blondie material, formed by the ex-members of Smooch, a band that had imitated Kiss in full makeup and regalia till the Kiss fad faded. It was driving Toni nuts, as they had insisted she dye her hair blonde, with a brunette patch in back, so she'd become a Debbie Harry clone. And even though she knew it was her fate, right now at least, to sing a lot of Blondie songs, enough was enough. Jon had grabbed her, had somehow got together with Les, Roc, and Mick, and had turned Deep Pink into the Nodes and hit the road.

"We got a week to kill," Toni was saying, "before the tryout in St. Paul. We going to visit your pal? What's his name?"

"Nolan, you mean."

"Yeah. Nolan. I'd like to meet that guy. We going to stay with him in Iowa City this week, or what?"

"He doesn't live there anymore. He moved."

"Oh, yeah? What about that place of yours, that antique shop your uncle left you?"

"I leased it to an old girlfriend of mine. She sells water beds."

"Oh, yeah, I remember her. The thirty-year-old hippie."

"All hippies are thirty years old now. Anyway, Karen's all right. She's got a kid I hate, but she's all right."

Roc's guitar screeched out there; guys in the audience hollered.

"Christ, his guitar playing bores me," Toni said, making a face, swigging some more whiskey. She drank a lot, but Jon never saw it take any noticeable effect.

"I did see somebody out there, you know," Jon said.

"Oh? If it's a girlfriend, I'd be jealous, if you and me were still an item."

"Two weekends ago we were an item. Kind of."

"Yeah, well, we're still friends, Jonny. If you don't have anything lined up, and I don't have anything lined up, we can still be an item anytime you feel like, far as I'm concerned. But you and I both know there's nothing serious in it for us."

He smiled. "You got nice tits, Toni. I'm real serious when it comes to your tits."

She uncrossed her legs, smiled at him. Gestured at him with the bottle of Cutty Sark. "C'mere, handsome."

He went to her. Gave her a little kiss. She draped her arms around his neck; the whiskey bottle was against his back.

"Want to be an item tonight?" she asked. "Want to be an item all next week? I got nothing better to do. How about you?"

"I got nothing planned."

"Unless it has to do with that old girlfriend you spotted."

He moved away from her.

"Hey," Toni said. "Something *is* wrong. What?"

Roc's guitar was screaming at the audience; the audience was screaming back.

"Nothing. I don't know. You know what I told you about? About me and Nolan, I mean."

"You told me a lot about you and Nolan."

"I shouldn't have."

"Well, you did."

"Well, I shouldn't have. You know what I'm talking about."

"I think I do. The robberies."

"The robberies and what went with it."

She screwed the cap back on the whiskey bottle, then hopped down off the amplifier flight case. "The guns and stuff," she said.

Jon laughed. "Yeah. The guns and stuff. Right. Well, I saw somebody from one of the things Nolan and I were into. One of the robberies."

"Somebody you robbed, you mean? Somebody who could recognize you?"

"Somebody that could recognize me, all right. Not somebody we robbed. Not hardly."

"Scratch fever . . . Cat scratch . . ."

"Somebody that was in it with you," she said. "Right."

"So?"

"So it was somebody that was supposed to have died in a car crash, a year ago."

"Jesus. What's that mean?"

"It means . . . I don't know what it means."

"Maybe your friend would. Nolan."

"Maybe."

"You thinking about calling him?"

"Yeah. I am."

"You better do it on the break. Those assholes are almost finished 'making pussies purr.'"

Out in the other room, on stage, the trio was doing its big finish, which amounted to lots of sliding up and down on the bass neck for Les, some horrible high squealing lead up on the neck of the Gibson Explorer for Roc, and a frantic series of trips around the drum kit for Mick.

"Let me have a sip of that," Jon said, nodding at her whiskey bottle.

"You never touch this shit," Toni said, unscrewing the cap again.

"I know," Jon said, taking the bottle, swigging it. "But Nolan does."

Soon they were back on stage doing a song called "Die Young, Stay Pretty."

2

IT WAS that kid, it was that goddamn kid!

Dammit!

What the hell was he doing here, playing in a rock band, for Christ's sake? His curly hair was shorter, but otherwise he hadn't changed; it was him, all right. Standing behind a portable organ, singing some unintelligible lyrics into a microphone, his voice booming out of the PA system.

The ironic thing was that it was this band—the Nodes—that had brought her here. She had heard the group was breaking up after this engagement, which meant they wouldn't have anything booked for the following week, which meant hopefully she could convince them to stay together long enough to play Tuesday through Saturday at her club, the Paddlewheel. She'd had a cancellation and needed a band, and this group, the Nodes, while not precisely the sort of group she usually booked in, had a reputation in the Midwest. So she'd come to hear them, and to talk to the leader.

Whose name, it turned out, was Jon.

"Yeah," Bob Hale said, as they sat at the bar on one side of the dance floor, yelling to be heard above the band, "it's that kid on the end, playing the organ."

She had looked at the kid, and he immediately seemed familiar to her.

"Nice enough kid," Bob was saying. He was a big, florid man in his forties, with reddish-brown hair and a childlike manner that gave him a certain immature charm. "You wouldn't know it to look at the squirt, but he's strong. Judas Priest, you should see him carry those amplifiers around, like they was pillows. The girls seem to go for him."

"Do they."

"Sure do." Bob grinned at her; he had big teeth. "Get you a drink, honey?"

"What did you say his name was?"

"Jon. I don't know what his last name is."

"Jon."

"Yeah. They're booked out of Des Moines. Or they were. Like I said, this is supposed to be their last night. But maybe I could talk to 'em for you and convince 'em that . . ."

She didn't hear anything else Bob said after that; she was walking away. Before that kid on stage got a good look at her.

Not that it mattered, at this point; she'd seen the flash of recognition—or *something*—on his face. He shouldn't have been able to recognize her, not at that distance; not with the blonde-streaked hair, the glasses, the business-like suit and sweater she'd worn. But the feeling in her stomach said he *had* recognized her. Goddammit. *Goddammit!*

Now she was out in the bar that connected the restaurant and club, which, like the rest of the Barn, was rustic—lots of rough barnwood decorated with an occasional horse-collar mirror and bogus wanted posters with Bob Hale's name and face on them. There were booths with baskets of peanuts and popcorn on either side of the dimly lit room, enclosed on three sides and affording enough privacy for people to sit and neck if they liked. Several couples were doing that now, and there were a few people sitting up at the bar, but otherwise the action at the Barn was clearly in where the Nodes were playing, rather obnoxiously, she thought. Which made her smile, and the smile felt like cement cracking. *If they play loud shit like that,* she thought, *I wouldn't have hired them anyway.*

She was sitting in a booth. The man she'd come with, Harold, looked over from the bar, where he was nursing a Scotch and water.

Harold was a big man, even though he stood only five-eight. He had the shoulders and thick arms, big hands, of a football player specifically a guard, which was the position he'd played in high school and college, before he dropped out. His face, however, was surprisingly sensitive: heavy-lidded gray eyes behind black-rimmed glasses; a bulbous, flat-bridged nose that had never been broken; a full-lipped, sensual mouth, kept wet by nervous licking.

He came over to her. He was wearing a tan suit with a dark tie; his hair, a sandy brown, was thinning on top and cut short on the sides. He looked like a high school football coach who quit to sell insurance; but what he was was her business partner, co-manager of the Paddlewheel, their club in Gulf Port.

"What's wrong?" Harold said. He had a soft, hoarse voice.

"Sit down," she said.

Harold had left his Scotch and water behind; he sat across from her, hands folded. He licked his lips. He had that look she hated: the look as if he were about to cry.

"I should've gone to fucking Brazil," she said. She was sitting shelling peanuts but not eating them.

"I see."

"Give me one good reason why I should ever have gone back to you."

"Okay. I love you."

"Shut up."

"What's wrong?"

"Nothing. Nothing I can't handle."

"I see."

"Do you?"

"I think so."

"Tell me, then."

"You saw somebody. Somebody who knew you, before."

"How could you know that?" She never failed to be surprised by the big jerk's perceptiveness.

"It was bound to happen," he said with a shrug, hands still folded, "sooner or later. We're not that far from where you lived before."

She tore the shell off a peanut, rubbed the skin off the nut within. Added it to the little pile she was making.

"You should leave," he was saying. "Have you spoken to this person?"

"No."

"Then you should leave. Leave while he or she still is wondering whether it was you or not It's that simple."

She threw a shell at him. "It's *not* that simple. God, you make me sick sometimes."

"Who is it? Who recognized you?"

"A kid in the band."

"A kid in the band?"

"A kid in the band. Remember the guy Logan I told you about?"

Logan was the name she knew Nolan by.

"Of course I remember."

That kid in there, the organ player, that's Jon."

"Logan's partner."

"That's right."

"Who was in on the Port City thing."

"Right."

"I see."

"Quit saying that!"

"All right. What do you want me to do?"

"Go in there and see which kid I mean. Go in and get a look at him. He's the short kid with curly hair and a good build."

"Okay."

"Then come back and sit in this booth and watch the door." The double doors between the bar and dance area were just a few feet away. "If he comes out and tries to use that pay phone during the band's break, stop him."

"How?"

"Just do it. But don't come on like a strongarm. Say you're expecting a call or something."

"All right. Then what?"

"Then nothing. Just keep an eye on him, when he isn't on stage. The band only has one more break. They're playing their third set now, which means they have one more set to play."

"After that, what happens?"

"We'll deal with that when the time comes."

"How?"

"However we have to."

He reached for the ashtray and with one thick hand brushed the pile of peanuts and shells she'd been making into it. Then he reached out and touched her hand. Held it.

"I don't kill people, Julie," he said softly. Eyes and lips wet.

"I know you don't."

"I'll do anything for you but that"

"I know you will."

"Anything."

"I know."

"But if it comes to . . . if it comes to that, I don't even want to know about it."

She smiled at him sweetly, squeezed his hand, thinking, *Fucking hypocrite! You don't care if somebody else does the killing, though, do you? Just so you don't have to do it; just so you don't have to know about it.*

She let go of his hand. "Give me some change. I have a long-distance call to make."

He half-stood in the booth, dug for some change, and gave it to her.

"Who are you calling?"

She got out of the booth. "You just stay put."

He licked his lips and nodded, then reached for the basket of peanuts.

She went over to the pay phone and dialed a number in Illinois direct.

It rang six times, then a slurry baritone voice came on, saying, "Yeah, what?"

"Ron?"

"Yeah."

"This is Julie."

"I know it is."

"I need you."

"Do you?"

"I have a problem."

"No kidding."

"I'm serious, Ron."

"So you're serious. I ain't heard from you in three weeks, and you're serious."

"I'm sorry. I really am."

"Why should I be surprised you're in trouble? You only come to me when you're in trouble."

"That isn't so."

"You only come to me when there's some shit job that old numb-nuts Harold won't do for you."

"Ron, you have to come here right away."

"Where's 'here'?"

"The Barn. Outside of Burlington."

"Yeah, I know the place. They got good rock 'n' roll there sometimes. Isn't this the Nodes' last weekend? That's a good band. Better than the shit you book in, anyway."

"Ron. This is serious."

"Yeah, okay. I can hear it in your voice, it's serious. Do I need to bring anything?"

"I think so."

"That serious, huh? It'll cost you."

"Money's no problem."

"Who's talking about money?"

"Ron. I'll make this worth it for you. I promise."

"Yeah, okay. I'm on my way."

The phone clicked dead.

She shivered and hung up.

She went back to the booth and sat across from Harold, who was eating peanuts, slowly, methodically.

"Ron's coming," she said.

"I see," he said. He pushed the basket of peanuts aside.

"Well, I can't depend on *you*, can I? If something ugly has to happen, Ron'll be up to it."

"How can you . . ."

"Because I have to," she said, biting off the words. "I'm supposed to be dead, goddammit . . . I ended up with $750,000 because Logan and Jon *thought* I was dead. If that kid gets to his friend with the news that I'm alive, that S.O.B.'ll come looking for me, *and* his money."

"I could handle him."

She laughed. "You couldn't handle Ron."

"Don't make fun of me, Julie."

"Harold, I'm sorry. You just don't know this guy Logan. He's like something out of a Mafia movie. Really scary."

"You've got money, Julie. Give him his share."

"He wouldn't be satisfied with just his share."

"Why not?"

"He's a killer. He tried to kill me, once, remember?"

That was a lie, of course; it had been the other way around, but Harold didn't know that.

Harold was balling those thick hands into fists the size of softballs. "If he tries to hurt you, I'll . . ."

"What? What will you do? You don't kill people, remember?"

They could hear the muffled blare of the band in the other room: *"Scratch fever . . . Cat scratch . . ."*

"That would be different," he said.

"Would it?"

"You know it would."

"We'll let Ron handle it."

"But who'll handle Ron?"

"I will."

"Good luck."

She could handle Ron, all right, but the price was high: letting those hands rove across her body; letting those lips do what they wanted to. Sharing a bed with Harold was bad enough. Getting in bed with Ron was flat-out disgusting.

And, deep down, she was afraid of Ron. She was afraid of few human beings on this earth, but Ron was one of them.

But then, so was the man she knew as Logan.

3

THE LAST SONG of the third set was "19th Nervous Breakdown," an old Stones song that Jon sang, and that tonight he was really identifying with.

He came down off the stage covered with sweat—not from nervousness: he was always wringing wet by the end of a set— and headed for the stage-right cubby hole behind the fake storefront, where he and Toni had spoken earlier. He grabbed a towel from the stack the Nodes always brought along with them. He wiped his face with it, rubbed his hair. Took off his shirt and ran the towel over his chest and back and arms, then put on a clean shirt. He went through at least three a night, and his sportcoat was always sopping by the end of the first set, discarded midway through the second. He worked hard at rock 'n' roll.

So did Toni, but she didn't seem to sweat at all. She stood in the doorway of the little room, leaning against the jamb, perverted pixie smile on her face. "How you doin'?" she asked him.

"Okay." Jon smiled back.

She came in and reached behind the amp and drum cases for her bottle of Cutty Sark. "Still got that old girlfriend on your mind?"

"Yeah."

She unscrewed the cap, swigged at the bottle. "Really sure it was her, are you?"

"I don't know. Maybe it wasn't."

Toni put the Cutty Sark away and took him by the arm. "Let's go have a look around."

Jon and Toni went out into the club and walked onto the dance floor. Les, Roc, and Mick were at a table, huddled together, making plans for the next incarnation of their band. The two factions of the Nodes didn't even exchange glances.

Their sound man/roadie, a twenty-year-old ex-DJ named Tommy, approached Jon and Toni. He looked like a pudgy, slightly dense Paul McCartney; he wore jeans and a T-shirt with the band's logo on it—the nodes—in Art Deco lettering.

"Good set," Tommy told them, smiling and nodding, on his way to join the Les, Roc, Mick faction, of which he was a part. Since he got his paychecks from Jon, however, Tommy stayed civil where Jon and Toni were concerned.

From the back of the hall, where the stage was, to the other end was nearly the length of a football field, and Jon and Toni were stopped a dozen times as they walked along the edge of the dance floor, by the crowded tables. The Nodes had played the Barn three times before, and had a following here; word had gotten around that this was the band's last night, and the fans were complaining.

A table of girls who had all gotten in on fake I.D.'s grabbed at Jon as he passed; arms, hands reached out for him, like *Night of the Living Dead*, only pretty.

"You can't break up," a little blonde in a red satin warm-up jacket and Clash T-shirt said. She had him by the arm.

A pudgy but cute brunette in a blue satin warm-up jacket and T-shirt that said "Wanna Party?" had him by the leg; she was saying something too, but Jon couldn't make it out

Two guys dressed like urban cowboys (and looking ridiculous, Jon thought, probably a couple of high school teachers who ditched their wives for the night) were standing talking to Toni, saying much the same thing the girls were saying to Jon, but without the touching. Relations between men and women may have changed, Jon noted, but it was still the women who did the touching without permission.

Bob Hale was still sitting on a stool over at the bar, stage right. Jon pulled away from the table of girls and went over to him, leaving Toni behind with her admirers in cowboy hats.

Bob extended a big, rough hand, which Jon shook.

"We're gonna miss you boys," Bob said. Considering the way Bob was always pursuing Toni, it was amazing he had included her as one of the "boys." Then, with a conspiratorial wink, Bob leaned in and said, "No other band pulls in the pussy like you guys." Bob was grinning like a junior high kid who'd just discovered *Hustler* magazine.

"I appreciate that, Bob," Jon said, sitting on the stool next to him. "You know, the other guys in the band'll still be together, under another name."

"I don't give a shit about those guys. They play too fuckin' loud. It's you and little Toni that go over. The pussies like *you*, and the guys go for *her*."

That was nice to hear, and was true enough, but Roc, Mick, and Les had a following, too. But Jon went along with Bob, saying, "Well, Toni and I may have a new band ourselves in a while."

"You just give me a call when you do, and you got a booking."

"Thanks, I will. Say, Bob. Who was that good-looking blonde you were talking to?"

"You'll have to narrow 'er down," Bob said, grinning even wider; he was the kind of person who could make a caricature out of himself without trying. "I talked to half a dozen good-looking blondes tonight already."

"This one is old enough to be in here legally."

"Yeah, but is she old enough for me to be in her legally?"

"She was about thirty, wearing a white jacket and dress, black sweater. Nice tits."

"Oh, yeah, her. She'll never drown."

"Right, well, I didn't get a good look at her from the stage. Aw, but you know how it is, Bob. Sometimes the closer you get . . ."

"The worse they look! Damn if that ain't the truth."

"How does this one look, close up?"

"Well she ain't a ten."

"No?"

"She's a thirteen."

"No kidding. Who is she? Do you know her?"

"Yeah, I know her. Wish I could say I could fix you up with her, but I never been able to get anywhere with her myself, believe it or not. That's a high-class cunt. She's got money."

"Really?"

"Yeah. Name's Julie something. She runs a place called the Paddlewheel, near Gulf Port."

"Illinois, you mean? Across from Burlington?"

Gulf Port was a wide-open little town where the bars stayed open all night. When clubs on the Iowa side shut down at two, the "Wanna Party?" die-hards headed for Gulf Port.

"Right," Bob said. "Quite a place. Big gambling layout and everything."

"You're shitting me."

"I wouldn't shit a shitter. Little Las Vegas, they call it. You oughta see the place. Maybe you will—she wanted to talk to you about that, in fact."

"This Julie did?"

"Yeah. She needs a band. Somebody cancelled out on her. She was hoping you guys might want one last job, 'fore you call it quits."

"No kidding. Well, maybe I ought to talk to her."

"That's the funny part. She was asking me about the band— asked about you, in particular—then she just walked away. I wasn't even through talking yet."

Jon smiled at Bob; inside his head sirens were going off and red lights were flashing. "Well, be honest, Bob—when are you ever through talking?"

"Ain't that the truth," Bob said, and slapped the bar, and drinks all down the line spilled a little.

Jon thanked Bob and went back to Toni, pulling her away from her admirers.

"I was right," he said, taking her by the arm.

"About what?"

"It was who I thought it was."

"The woman?"

"Yes." And he told her what Bob had told him.

"So what now?"

"Now I call Nolan."

The pay phone was in the bar, on the wall around the corner from the pinball machines. He got change from the bartender. Toni was right with him.

"Do you have this guy's number?" she asked.

"Yeah. I memorized it."

"Memorized it?"

"In case something like this came up."

"Oh."

He had the receiver up to his ear and the coins poised to drop, when a hand settled on his shoulder, like a UFO landing. It was a hand that made Bob Hale's hand seem dainty.

Jon turned and looked at a guy just a few inches taller than he was but infinitely bigger. A sandy-haired man with sad grey eyes behind dark-rimmed glasses, and shoulders you had to look at one at a time.

"Excuse me," the man said. He licked his lips.

"Yeah?"

"I'm waiting for an important call."

"My call won't take long."

"I'd appreciate it if you'd not use the phone."

It wasn't a threat, exactly; the tone was rather kind—*Please do me a favor*. But the favor was being asked by a man who looked like the son of Kong in a business suit.

"Look," Jon said, "this is a public phone. You can't keep people from using it."

Which was a ridiculous thing to say. This guy could obviously keep people from using the phone. He could keep the state of Iowa from using the phone.

"I have a sick kid," the man said. Softly. "I'm waiting to hear about my sick kid."

Toni spoke up. "What the fuck are you doing here, then?"

Jon raised a hand to quiet her. "It's okay, Toni." He smiled at the guy. "It's no emergency on my end, mister. You can wait for your call. Be my guest."

Toni stood with fists on hips and glared at Jon, who pulled her away from there by the arm.

"Jon, why are you letting that asshole . . ."

"Shut up," Jon said, and took her back into the club.

He pulled her off into another of the cubbyhole rooms behind the storefronts; a couple was making out in this one, so Jon dragged her into the cubbyhole next door. She was fuming.

"Why d'you go along with that bullshit?" she demanded.

"I think somebody told him not to let me use the phone."

Toni thought about that

"Look," he said. "I got to find out if that woman is still around. My guess is she split, but if she's still around, maybe I could corner her or something. I don't know."

"What good'll that do?"

"Maybe I can avoid a violent confrontation. I know how this woman's mind works. She'll figure if Nolan finds out she's alive, he'll come looking for her."

"Is she right?"

"Yeah."

"So what good does talking to her do?"

"I'll lie. I'll tell her Nolan's dead or in prison or something. That she has nothing to worry about from him."

"But what about from you?"

"I'll tell her I don't give a damn, personally, about her or the money she took."

"Is that true?"

"No."

"Well, let's go look for her, then."

They went back out through the bar, and noticed that the sandy-haired guy was sitting in a booth near the double doors to the club area, well around the corner from the pay phone, not an ideal place for somebody waiting for a call. Jon looked at him with a smile and a silent question, and he looked back and shook his head no, indicating that the call hadn't come yet. Jon shrugged at him, smiled again, and walked on with Toni.

Around the corner, a drunk in overalls was leaning against the wall, talking on the phone, slobbering at the receiver.

Jon said, "Looks like I'm the only one the worried papa wants to keep off the phone."

He and Toni casually walked through the bar and up through the restaurant, both floors of it, and the woman with streaked blonde hair and tinted glasses wasn't there.

"She either split," Jon said, "or she's outside, ducking me. In her car in the parking lot, maybe."

"You want to go looking for her?"

"Not in a dark parking lot."

"You're not scared of her?"

"Of course I am."

"Why?"

"She almost killed me once. With a shotgun."

"Oh." Toni swallowed and followed Jon back into the club, where they immediately headed for Bob Hale, still perched at the stage-right bar.

"Bob," Jon said, putting a good-buddy hand on the big man's shoulder, "some drunk is tying up the pay phone."

"Well," Bob said, smiling, hauling himself off the stool, "let's kick his ass off, then."

"No, no. Listen, I have a kind of private call I'd like to make. Can I use the phone in your apartment?"

Bob grinned at Jon, then at Toni, then back at Jon. "You two can use my apartment for anything you want, if I can watch."

21

Toni laughed—a little tensely, but she laughed. She liked Bob, Jon knew. Considered him harmless, a teddy bear with a hard-on.

"No, really," Jon said, "I need to use the phone. How about it?"

"Sure," Bob said, and led them back around the bar to a hallway. They followed him down it.

Bob lived at the Barn. So did a German Shepherd about the same size as Jon. It stayed in the bedroom Bob kept, on the lower floor of the barn part of the Barn, in the rear, a bedroom Bob referred to as his apartment.

Bob unlocked the door, and the dog began to growl. It sounded like Mt. St. Helen's thinking it over. Bob reached a hand down and grabbed the dog by the collar and pulled him away from the doorway, back into the bedroom. The dog was still growling, but that only made Bob laugh. Amid the laughter, he gave the dog a sharp command, and the dog sat, teeth bared, Rin Tin Tin with rabies. If Bob hadn't been there, Jon and/or Toni would have been dead by now.

It was a big, messy room: plush red carpeting with underwear, shirts, other clothing carelessly wadded and tossed; a queen-size canopy waterbed with red satin sheets and black plush covers over at the right. No rough barn wood here: dark paneling, with built-in closet. At the near end was a bookcase wall with no books in it, just thousands of dollars' worth of stereo equipment, as well as a 19-inch Sony with videotape deck, and a library of XXX tapes.

Also the phone, which Bob handed Jon as he marched the dog out into the hall, closing the door as he went. Toni stood and watched as Jon touch-toned Nolan's number.

On the third ring, he heard Nolan's voice: "This is Nolan."

"Nolan! Listen . . ."

"You're talking to a machine. Leave your message at the beep."

Jon just looked at the phone.

"What's wrong?" Toni said.

"An answer machine," he said. "Now I've heard everything. Nolan's got an answer phone! I don't believe this."

The phone said, *beep*.

Jon left his message, Bob locked his dog back in the bedroom, and they all went back into the club, where Jon and Toni headed for the stage.

For the last set.

4

WHEN SHE blew the words on "Heartbreaker," Toni *knew* she was scared.

Certainly not stage fright—she'd been singing with rock bands since junior high—but some *other* kind of scared, something in her stomach that was far worse than butterflies.

Something cold.

Something alive.

Fear.

When the song was finished, she rushed over to Jon and whispered, "Fill in with something. I need a few minutes."

Jon nodded, and away from the mike, stage-whispered to Les, Roc, and Mick to "forget the list—do 'Light My Fire' next," a song Toni didn't do anything on, which would give her a chance to take a break.

She stood inside the cubbyhole room stage right as the band went into the old Doors classic, Jon doing right by the elaborate pseudo-baroque organ break at the beginning. She was breathing hard. She wanted a smoke. She'd given it up two years ago and rarely had felt the urge since the first hard months, but now she wanted a smoke. She went out and bummed one off Tommy, the roadie, sitting at his sound board halfway down the dance floor, over stage left. Then she returned to the cubbyhole, sucking in smoke as if it was food and she was starving.

Mick was singing. He didn't sing very well, and in fact was

incurably flat, but the Doors tune lent itself to that: the late Jim Morrison was known for many things, but singing on key wasn't one of them. Then the band went into the instrumental section of the song, Jon taking the organ solo, a sing-song thing that climbed the scale in mindless little would-be Bach progressions.

She wondered if that big sandy-haired guy—Jesus, was he big—was still in his booth, waiting for his mythical phone call. She decided to find out. She'd have plenty of time; this song went on for nearly ten minutes. She wandered back through the club, nodding as fans touched her arm and made comments about the sad fact that the Nodes were splitting, and then she was in the bar, where the big sandy-haired guy was sitting in the booth, talking intensely with a woman.

A woman in white with a black cardigan and tinted glasses and a beautiful face and—even seated in a booth it was obvious—a beautiful body.

Suddenly the cigarette was burning her throat I knew *there was a reason I quit these fucking things*, she thought, and went up to the bar and put the cig out in an ashtray up from the bottom of which a little picture of Bob Hale stared. Standing next to her at the bar were two young women.

Toni had seen these women before; they had been to hear the Nodes at the Ramp in Burlington a few months ago, part of a group of half a dozen hard, hoody-looking bitches, one of whom had been attracted to Jon, and vice versa. She was one of the two at the bar, a lanky brunette about nineteen, in jeans and jeans jacket and a Nodes T-shirt; lots of eye makeup, and smoking a cigarette.

The other woman was in her early twenties, medium height, boyish build—nothing remarkable, other than the close-set beady eyes, the lump of a nose, the thick lips with permanent, humorless sneer, the dishwater blonde hair greased back in a ducktail, the black leather jacket and red T-shirt and jeans, cigarette dangling from the Presleyesque lips, a hand on the other girl's shoulder.

Toni couldn't remember their names, but she did remember that the night Jon and the brunette had spent a break in the band's van, the beauty with the ducktail had come up and smiled at Jon during the next break and, cleaning her nails with a switchblade, told Jon if he ever touched Darlene (*that* was the first girl's name; what was the second one's?) again, she would cut his balls off and hang 'em over her rearview mirror. Jon hadn't argued with her. He'd tried to make a joke out of it later, about what a cornball creep that dyke was, doing her Sha Na Na routine. But it hadn't come off: Jon knew the dyke had meant what she said.

Terrific, Toni thought It wasn't enough somebody shows up from the part of Jon's past that included that thief Nolan; the dyke and Darlene had to turn up, too. Wonderful.

She ducked back into the club. Jon was still playing his organ solo, getting ready to let Roc take over on guitar.

"Light My Fire" — the baroque opening, anyway — had been the first thing she'd ever heard Jon play on the organ. She'd been in a music store in Iowa City — the Sound Pit — looking at PA equipment with some of those jerks in her old band, Dagwood, and Jon was playing a Crumar portable organ, asking the clerk if he knew anywhere he could find an old Vox Super Continental. The clerk was trying to sell Jon a Moog synthesizer, telling him *nobody* played combo organ anymore, and Jon was saying, "Bullshit, the punk and new wave bands are *all* using old Vox and Farfisas."

When she heard that she knew she'd found a kindred spirit. She started up a conversation with him, and soon they were having a drink at the Mill, a bar in downtown Iowa City, and then they were in bed at his apartment, or anyway the room he kept on the bottom floor of the antique shop he'd inherited from his uncle, a shop that had been closed since the uncle's death.

Rock 'n' roll, it seemed, was not Jon's first love. He lived in a cartoonist's studio, with drawing board, boxes of comic books, posters of comic strip characters like Dick Tracy and Batman and Tarzan, some framed original strips, making a gray-walled, cement-floored former storeroom a four-color shrine to comic art. Even the finely carved antique headboard of the bed they were in had some drawings tacked to it — Jon's own work, and good work it was, at that.

"Are you a musician or a cartoonist or what?" she'd asked him, letting the sheet fall to her waist as she turned to look at his drawings; she liked her breasts and liked having him look at them as she looked at his art.

"I don't know if I'm either anymore," he said. He was sitting up in bed with a pillow propped behind him. His chest was almost completely hairless, she noted.

"What do you mean by that?"

"I've been at this cartooning shit for as long as I can remember."

"Oh, and you're all of twenty."

"Twenty-one. I'd guess that's about how old you are, too. And I bet you aren't finding rock 'n' roll an easy life, either."

"You're right," she admitted. "I been at it eight years, and it's a hard go, even if you're good at it, and I am."

"Yeah, well, I'm good at cartooning and I'm not making it."

"It's hard to make it in any of the arts."

"No kidding. Oh, I've had a couple of things published in the undergrounds. Ever hear of *Bizarre Sex*?"

She smiled. "Try me."

"That's the name of an underground comic. I've done a couple of science fiction parody things for 'em. Doesn't pay much."

"It's a start."

"But it isn't a career. I don't know. I don't have much interest in commercial art, and the comic book field doesn't appeal to me; the pay sucks and they're doing the same old superhero junk, only badly."

"What about a newspaper comic strip?"

"Landing a syndicated strip is almost impossible, particularly if you don't do humor, which I don't."

"I thought you said you did two parodies for that underground comic."

"Yeah, but I doubt many newspapers would want to carry 'Dildos in Space.'"

"You may have a point. So where does music come in?"

"What do you mean?"

"I heard you play the organ. You're good."

"Aw, that's nothing serious with me. I played off and on with some bands when I was in junior high and high school. I don't think I could make a living at it. And I'm not sure I'd want to, if I could."

"Why?"

"My mother was in 'show biz,' and she had a shitty life, playing piano and singing in bars, on the road all the time, dreaming of being on Ed Sullivan someday, only he's dead now, and so is she."

"Do you have any kids?"

"Kids? Me? Hell, no."

"Then you wouldn't be doing anybody a disservice leaving 'em behind when you went on the road, would you? If that's what your problem is."

He thought about that a while. Then he said, "What kind of band would I be in? I hate disco. I hate country rock. I hate heavy metal. There isn't much I could stand to play, except old sixties stuff and maybe some of the new wave music coming out of England and the East Coast."

And that had been the beginning of it. She had told him about her mock-Blondie band, Dagwood, which she wanted out of, and together they made plans to launch what became the Nodes. She knew about Roc, Mick, and Les, and they all got together in a friend's garage and jammed through some material, and two weeks later they had relocated in Des Moines, to be with the booking agency that had handled the now-defunct Dagwood.

Leaving Iowa City for Des Moines seemed to be slightly rough for Jon. He didn't say much about it but he was apparently very close to this guy Nolan, though they seemed to have had a minor falling-out of some kind lately, which made it easier to Jon to leave. So he said, anyway.

She had only seen this Nolan a few times. Actually, he seemed to be using the name Logan, but Jon always referred to him as Nolan. She didn't know if Nolan had ever even noticed her, really; to him she was probably just some twat Jon was shacking up with. They'd never exchanged a word.

But she had noticed him, all right. Looked him over good.

He was handsome, in an ugly way. A big, lean man with the slightest paunch, with dark, somewhat shaggy hair that was graying at the temples, and widow's peaked. He had high cheekbones, a mustache, and a mean look, but those eyes, those narrow, squinting eyes, had something else in them besides meanness. Intelligence, for sure. Humanity? Humor? Maybe not.

At the time, Nolan had been running some sort of restaurant in Iowa City, in which Jon was a partner, it seemed, though he didn't say much about that. When she saw Nolan, he'd be dressed in a sportcoat and turtleneck and slacks, something casual, in a country club sort of way, and the guy looked good, looked right. Only something was wrong; something about him made her think of a gangster.

She used to kid Jon about that.

"I wonder what your gangster friend's doing right now," she'd say, sitting up in bed in a motel room, watching TV, on the road with the Nodes.

"Probably sticking up a bank," Jon would answer, with a funny smile.

She and Jon had continued to share a room on the road, even though their romance had turned into a friendship, albeit a friendship that included sleeping together (but only occasionally screwing) and getting out of each other's way when an attractive member of the opposite sex came along. She had a feeling Jon could have been serious about her if she let him, but her insistence that she was not a one-man woman, that marriage and whatever were not in her plans ever, cooled him off a bit.

And he did seem to like the freedom to go after the bitches, like that Darlene she'd spotted out in the bar. Jon was a weird kid, in a way, so goddamn straight. He didn't even smoke dope—no drugs at all; no booze to speak of, either.

There was that one time, however, that he got good and plastered. It was at a party at some trailer out in the country, where a guy had a hog roast at three in the morning after the Nodes had played a particularly long night at a particularly rowdy bar. The girl Jon was with, a short little blonde in halter top and jeans, was the sort who wanted to drink but would not drink alone, and so Jon drank with her and later crawled off into the woods with her, too. But by the time he ended up back at the motel with Toni, he was plastered—plastered in the way that only someone who doesn't get plastered often can get plastered. And he started to talk.

And he told her the damnedest things.

About him and Nolan.

And bank robberies and shooting somebody called Sam Comfort, some crazy old man who was a thief himself who Jon and Nolan were looting, and wild goddamn things about some girl getting her head blown off by somebody called Gross, and shoot-outs in lodges up in Wisconsin. And the next morning Jon asked her to forget all that stuff he told her last night, and there had never been a word about it since.

Till tonight.

"Light My Fire" was almost over.

She got back up on stage, and Jon gave her a little smile and she gave him one back, nodding, and they went into the next song.

Playing tambourine and singing back-up, she glanced over at Jon, and he was into the music—not a sign of worry. And she felt better. Jon had left a message for Nolan, and the woman in white and her big sandy-haired stooge didn't know that. And that made Toni feel better; the cold feeling at the pit of her stomach was gone.

Then she noticed Jon flubbing the words on "Jailhouse Rock."

And at the back of the room, standing by the double doors, the big sandy-haired man waited and watched.

5

THEY GOT called back for two encores. One encore was typical for the Nodes; they were good enough to expect that. A second encore indicated to Jon that the word had spread through the crowd that this was the band's last night.

Some of Roc's followers were shouting for "Cat Scratch Fever" again, and even though Jon and Toni weren't featured on it, making it inappropriate for an encore, Jon went ahead and announced it and went off with Toni into the stage-right cubbyhole to wait it out.

"*That* fucking thing again," Toni said, shaking her head. Still not sweating.

"No accounting for taste," Jon said, smiling back.

"We better do one more and put this turkey out of its misery."

Jon nodded. "You okay?"

"I think so. I blew some words."

"I know you did. That's not like you."

"Yeah, well, I started thinking about the words, and that's deadly. As soon as you start thinking about 'em, you lose 'em."

"Right I blew a few myself. Lots of hamburger tonight."

Hamburger was garbled singing with the mouth right up against the mike, sounding like words but not words at all.

"Jon, that big guy's still hanging around. When I took that little break midway through the set, he was still sitting in his booth. Then he came and stood in back and watched for a while."

"Yeah, I know. I saw him."

"Yeah, well, your girlfriend was there, too."

"No kidding?"

"The one with the white outfit and the big tits? Yeah. Still here. Or she was twenty minutes ago, anyway."

"Jesus. So she didn't split."

"Nope. Somebody else was out there, too."

"Who?"

"Darlene."

"Who the fuck's Darlene?"

"You mean, which fuck's Darlene, don't you? Burlington, a couple of months ago? The Ramp? Lanky with brown hair and lots of eye makeup?"

"I think I remember."

"Had a dyke girlfriend who wanted to cut your nuts off?"

"I remember."

"Well, she's out there, too, cuter than Rod Stewart's mom. What's that dyke's name, anyway?"

"I don't remember."

"Me either. So, Jonny. Tonight's a real stroll down memory lane, for you, huh? Maybe they're all here 'cause it's the Nodes' last night."

"Maybe."

"Are you scared?"

"A little."

"Yeah. Me too. I'd take another hit of Cutty Sark if I thought I could keep it down. What should we do?"

"Get back on stage and play one more song, I guess."

They did—"Johnny B. Goode" by Chuck Berry.

And it was the last song the Nodes ever played together, because the audience was too worn out and drunk to work up the applause for another encore, and Jon and Toni and the rest of the band came down off the stage and mingled with the crowd, as the Barn would be open for another half-hour before the lights would come up and the band's equipment would get torn down. The jukebox started up and an Olivia Newton-John record came on, a mild protest by someone not into the Nodes' brand of hard-core rock 'n' roll. Couples slow danced. Singles who hadn't scored shuffled toward exits, looking around one last time to see if somebody was left to come onto.

First order of business at the end of a performance was getting paid, and since Jon was listed as leader on the union contract Bob Hale had signed, it was Jon who followed Bob back behind the bar again, through a hallway and into a small office. Bob paid Jon in cash, shook his hand, reminded him to keep in touch if he and Toni put another band together, and went back to the table out in the club where a short-haired brunette waitress with a slender figure and a tired, pretty face waited to be the queen of Bob's waterbed this winter night.

Usually Jon waited till later to pay off the band members, but tonight he gathered them in the stage-right cubbyhole and gave them their shares, holding back his one-and-a-half shares (he owned the PA equipment and van and so got an extra half-share) as well as the agent's commission. These five people had worked and lived together for some seven months, and despite their differences, this was an awkward if not exactly poignant moment.

Roc scratched the side of his narrow, faintly pockmarked face; he had some eye makeup on, which had always looked silly to Jon before. Now, for some unknown reason, Jon felt touched by the guitarist's show-bizzy affectation, out here in the Iowa sticks.

Roc extended his hand, and he and Jon—the two strong ones in the group, whose conflicting tastes had made this split inevitable—shook hands in a sideways, "soul" shake.

"It's been real," Roc (whose real name was Arnold) said, with a small, embarrassed smile.

"It's been real," Jon agreed, giving him back the same kind of smile.

There was a brief round of handshakes; the boys, except for Jon, each gave Toni a hug. Mick advised her to "watch the sauce—it'll catch up with you someday," and she advised him to "watch that dope you smoke or you'll wake up even dumber some morning," and they all laughed.

"We're not going to tear our stuff down tonight," Roc told Jon. "Bob said we could come back tomorrow and do it."

"I figured as much," Jon said. He knew that they planned to rent a trailer to haul their amps and guitars away. Usually the band traveled in two vehicles: Jon's van, with all the major equipment and room for two riders (invariably, Jon and Toni) and Roc's station wagon, which held the other band members and a few odds and ends of equipment

"We'll help take the PA and mikes down, of course," Mick added. "Help you load your organ and stuff, if you want."

"I appreciate it," Jon said, and everyone left the little cubbyhole and wandered out onto the dance floor, where the lights had just come up, bringing the usual groans and moans from the crowd, who, like a mole caught in the headlights of a car, preferred the dark.

"What now?" Toni asked Jon.

"I think I'll see if the phone's free."

"You already left your message, didn't you?"

"Yeah. But I'd like to see if I can get through to Nolan, and not his machine. I'd also like to see if Julie and the Incredible Hulk are still around."

They walked toward the outer bar.

"What if they are?" Toni asked.

"If Julie's here, I want to talk to her. Like I said, maybe I can defuse this thing. If that guy's still around and she isn't, I'm curious to see if he'll let me use the phone."

"And if he won't?"

"I'll talk to Bob. He's got a dog and a shotgun."

They entered the bar; people were getting one last drink, but the booths on either side were empty—nothing but moisture rings and ashtrays full of peanut shells.

No Julie.

No Hulk.

"Let's look around some more," Jon said.

"Like outside?"

"Like outside."

They went out on the wooden sidewalk that ran in front of the building. The night was cold; they could see their breath. It was November and it hadn't snowed yet. People were getting into their frost-frosted cars, most of the couples hanging onto each other, some because they were drunk, others because they were horny, and in a lot of cases both. No sign of Julie or her Hulk.

"Let's go back in," Jon suggested, and they did.

They took a booth.

"I don't know what to make of this," he said. "I know she spotted me. Shit."

"You got word through to your friend," Toni said, sounding as though she were trying to convince herself as much as Jon. "Why worry about it?"

"What, me worry? Look, let's go tear down the stuff and get the van loaded; the guys'll help us, and maybe Bob and his people'll pitch in, and we can get it done fast and head for Nolan's."

"Maybe he's already on his way here."

"You got a point. I'll try him again."

He went to the phone. He had a dime poised to drop in the slot when a hand rested on his shoulder. Not a big hand this time, but a smaller, softer one.

He turned and looked at Darlene, whom he suddenly remembered very well. Her long brown hair was in a sixties shag, and she did have lots of eye makeup (even more than Roc); she reminded him of Chrissie Hynde, of the Pretenders. A smiling, skinny girl, taller than he was, with pert little breasts bobbling under a Nodes T-shirt; he couldn't remember that logo of his looking better.

She stroked his bare arm; he was wearing only a T- shirt, now, himself, also a Nodes T-shirt. She poked at the design on his chest, traced it with her finger.

"We look like twins," she said.

"Not quite," Jon said. "Hiya Darlene."

An image of that shaggy brunette hair buried in his lap flashed through his mind; the van back behind the Ramp. Oh yes.

"I'm sorry you guys are splitting up," she said. "You got a good band."

"We had a good band. It's over now."

"I'm sad."

"No big deal."

"I need a shoulder to cry on."

Your makeup'll run, he thought, annoyed with her and with himself, because she was making his jeans tight.

"You still got your van?"

"Sure, but right now I gotta help tear down, Darlene."

"This won't take long."

She had a whory mouth, but in a nice way, and though her teeth were faintly yellow, from smoking no doubt, they were nice teeth, and her tongue peeking out between the parted teeth was nice, too.

"How about another time?" Jon said. Polite smile.

"No time like the present." She had hold of his arm, hugging it, tugging at him.

He glanced back at Toni, in her booth; she was smiling at him, amused. But then she mouthed something at him. He couldn't make it out and squinted and Toni tried again: *What about the dyke?* she was silently saying.

Jon turned back to Darlene, said, "What about your friend?"

She was still tugging him along, toward the door. "You're my friend, Jon boy."

"Please don't call me Jon boy. This is not 'The Waltons.' This is definitely not 'The Waltons.'"

She laughed, as if she understood him. "Come on. I got a present for you."

Jon didn't smoke. Jon didn't drink. Jon didn't do dope. But Jon did have a weakness. And Darlene was definitely part of that weakness.

He went outside with her.

"I said, what about that girlfriend of yours?" he said, pulling loose from her, getting an arm's length between them.

"She's not here."

"Well she *was* here," he said. "I *saw* her." He hadn't, really, but Toni had.

"So she was here," she said, "so what? She's gone now."

"Well, isn't she your . . ."

"She's just another guy to me."

"So I gathered."

"Come on, I got something for you," she said, tugging him toward the van, which was parked way down at the end of the tin shed that was the club portion of the Barn. The Nodes logo on their T-shirts was also on the side of the van, painted there, frosted over at the moment. Hugging his arm, she pushed herself against him, snuggled against him. As they walked, their footsteps sounded hollow on the wooden sidewalk. When they spoke, their cold breath hung briefly in the air, as though the words themselves were hanging there.

"What's her name, anyway?" Jon said.

"Who?"

"Your girlfriend?"

"Who cares?"

They were at the van. Jon unlocked the side door and they got in. There were some blankets on the cold metal floor of the van, which were used as padding between the amplifiers and such when the van was loaded for travel, and were also used for occasions like this, with Jon and Darlene falling on top of each other in the back of the van.

"It's a little cold," Jon said, reaching over and locking the door they'd just come in. "Maybe I should turn on the heater."

"It won't be cold long," Darlene said, pulling her T-shirt off. Her nipples were two red bumps in pink circles riding small, high breasts above a bony ribcage; Jon put his hands on the breasts, kissed the breasts, but his heart wasn't in it. His hard-on wasn't, either. It was, in fact, gone.

Because all he could think of what that dyke, whose name he couldn't remember, not that it mattered. He wasn't even thinking about Julie and that Hulk of hers, really, it was that goddamn dyke. . . .

Then she was at his fly, and her head was in his lap again, and he was suddenly getting back into it when the side door of the van opened and Jon, angry, confused—*I* locked *that!*—said, "Shut that fucking thing!" and then saw who it was who opened it.

The dyke.

Terrific.

"Put your shirt on," the dyke said to Darlene. A low, but not exactly masculine voice.

Darlene, still blasé, did so, saying, "I only did what you told me to."

Like unlock the goddamn door when he wasn't looking, Jon thought, as the dyke crawled inside the van and shut the door behind her. In a black leather jacket and dishwater blonde ducktail and Elvis sneer, she was a fifties parody. A fifties nightmare.

"You don't scare me," Jon said, zipping up, scared. "Now just get out of here. Take your friend with you."

The dyke pulled at either side of her leather jacket, and the metal buttons popped open, and she took something out of her waistband. It was a gun. A revolver with a long barrel. Just like the one Nolan used.

"What is this? . . ." Jon started to say.

Just as the dyke was swinging the gun barrel around to hit him along the side of his head, the damnedest thing happened: he remembered her name.

Ron.

2

6

IT WAS a November afternoon that could have passed for September—not quite Indian summer, cooler than that, but with the sun visible in a blue, not quite cloudless sky. A nice day to be in Iowa City—if you liked Iowa City.

And Nolan didn't, particularly. Maybe that was why he moved out of here, a few months ago. That had certainly been part of it. That and Jon leaving.

Not that he and Jon had been particularly close. They had been through a lot together, but basically they were just partners—in crime, in business, if there was a difference—and had shared that old antique shop as mutual living quarters for a year or so. That was about the extent of it.

But without Jon around, Iowa City stopped making sense to Nolan. It was as though the town had an excuse being this way, with a kid like Jon living in it; now Nolan felt out of place, out of step, and more than a little bored in a college town perched uneasily between *Animal House* and Woodstock.

This downtown, for instance.

He was seated on a slatted wood bench. A few years ago, if he'd been sitting here, he'd have been run over: he'd have been sitting in the middle of a street. Since then, the street had been closed off so these college children could wander among wooden benches and planters and abstract sculptures, like the one nearby, a tangle of black steel pipe on a pedestal, an ode to plumbing, Nolan guessed. Some grade-schoolers were climbing on a wooden structure that was apparently supposed to be a sort of jungle gym; very "natural," organic as shit, he supposed, but the tykes seemed as confused by it as he was. A movie theater was playing something from Australia given four stars by a New York critic; people were lined up as if it was *Star Wars 12*. A boy and girl in identical U of I warm-up jackets strolled into a deep-pan pizza place; another couple, dressed strictly army surplus, followed soon after and would no doubt opt for "whole wheat" crust. Nolan hadn't seen so much khaki since he was in the service. One kid in khaki was playing the guitar and singing something folksy, as though he hadn't heard about Vietnam ending. Like Nolan, he was seated on a wood bench, and people huddled around and listened, applauding now and then, perhaps to keep warm. Nolan burrowed into his corduroy jacket, waiting for Wagner, feeling old.

That was it. Sudden realization: these kids made him feel old. Jon hadn't had that effect on him. Jon had, admittedly, looked up to him, in a way. But it hadn't made him feel old. Not this kind of old, anyway.

He glanced over at the bank. The time/temperature sign said it was 3:35. Wagner had been in there an hour-and-a-half already. Nolan had been in there, too, but only long enough to sign the necessary papers. He didn't feel comfortable in a bank unless he was casing or robbing it.

For nearly twenty years, Nolan had been a professional thief.

His specialty was the institutional robbery: banks, jewelry stores, armored cars, mail trucks. He had gone into that line more or less as a matter of survival. He had been employed in Chicago, by the Family, in a noncriminal capacity, specifically managing a Rush Street nightclub; but a falling out with his bosses (which included killing one of them) had sent him into the underground world of armed robbery.

Not that he'd been a cheap stick-up man. No, he was a pro— big jobs, well planned, smoothly carried out. Nobody gets hurt. Nobody goes to jail.

It took almost the full twenty years for those Family difficulties to cool off—then, largely due to a change of regime— and it was during those last difficult days of his Family feud that Nolan teamed up with Jon. An unlikely pairing: a bank robber pushing fifty and a comic-collecting kid barely twenty. But Jon was the nephew of Planner, the old goat who pretended to be in the antique business when what he really was was the guy who sought out and engineered jobs for men like Nolan. It had been at Planner's request that Nolan took the kid on.

And the kid had come through, these past couple of years— the two Port City jobs; the Family trouble that included Planner being murdered; the heisting of old Sam Comfort And more.

But Jon just wasn't cut out for crime. Oh, he was a tough little character, and no coward. He'd saved Nolan's life once. Nolan hadn't forgotten. But the kid had a conscience, and a little of that went a long way in Nolan's racket.

Fortunately, he and Jon had made enough good scores to retire, about a year ago. Or anyway, Nolan considered himself retired, knowing that his was a business you never got out of, not entirely; there were too many ties to the past for that.

Wagner was one of those ties: a boxman, a safecracker, who retired a few years ago and started up a restaurant in Iowa City, called the Pier. He'd made a real go of it but his health failed, and he invited Nolan to buy him out and Nolan had.

Only now Nolan was in the final stages of reversing that process: letting Wagner buy him out and take the Pier back over.

And there Wagner was—knifing through the crowd of window-shopping kids, moving way too fast for a guy in his fifties with a heart condition. But then, that was always Wagner's problem: he moved too fast, was too goddamn intense, a thin little nervous tic of a man with short white hair, a prison-grey complexion, and a flat, featureless face made memorable only by a contagious smile.

And then he was sitting next to Nolan, pumping Nolan's hand and saying, "You're a pal, Nolan, you're really a pal."

"I made money on the deal," Nolan said noncommittally.

"Not that much. Not that goddamn much. It was nice of him wasn't it?"

"Nice of who?"

"The banker!"

"Bankers aren't nice. Bankers are just bankers."

"It was nice of him, Nolan. To come down after hours to sign papers. That just isn't done, you know."

"Banks have been known to open at odd hours."

"Huh? Oh, yeah. I get it Ha! Lemme buy you lunch."

"It's past lunch."

"Why, did you eat already?"

"No."

"Then let's have lunch. It'll make a great prelim to dinner. It's on me, Nolan."

"Okay," he said.

They walked across the bricked former street to a place called Bushnell's Turtle; it was a sandwich place specializing in submarines (its name derived from the fact that a guy named Bushnell invented the "turtle," the first submersible) and was in a beautiful old restored building with lots of oak and stained glass and plants. They stood and looked at the menu, which was on a blackboard, and a guy in a ponytail and apron came and wrote their order down. Then they were in line a while; the kid in front of Nolan was long-haired and in overalls with a leather thong around his neck and was reading, while he waited, a book called *Make Your Own Shoes*. Soon they picked their food up at the old-fashioned soda-fountainlike bar, where the nostalgic spirit was slightly disrupted when a computer cash register totaled their order.

"The hippies did it right for once," Wagner said, referring to the restaurant. He was about to bite into a sub the size of one of the shoes the kid in line was planning to make.

"I agree with you," Nolan managed, between bites of a hot bratwurst sandwich, dripping with mozzarella cheese and sauerkraut.

"I love this town. Love it. Makes me feel young."

"Yeah, well, it makes me feel old, and you be careful or you'll have another heart attack before the ink is dry."

"Don't worry about me," he said, his mouth full of sub, "this pacemaker's made a new man out of me."

"You should've stayed in Florida. There's nothing wrong with being retired."

"Florida stinks! Nothing but old people and Cubans."

"And sunshine and girls in bikinis."

"Don't believe everything the Chamber of Commerce tells you. How's the Quad Cities thing working out?"

"Okay," Nolan said. "It's early yet."

"It's smaller than the Pier, I take it"

"Much. I can loaf with this place."

"You opened yet?"

"In a couple weeks. Still getting the inventory together. Still working with the staff."

"I'm sure you're working with the staff. Particularly the female staff."

"Just one." He smiled.

"Special, this one?"

"Just a girl. I knew her from before."

"Oh. What's it called?"

"Sherry."

"Not the girl, the joint."

"Nolan's."

"No kidding? What was it called before that?"

"I don't know. I think it was always called Nolan's. It's been around for years. That's why I had to shut it down, for remodeling and such."

"Whaddya know. It must've been meant to be. So are you using the Nolan name there, then?"

"Yeah. I decided to. The coincidence of it was just too good to pass up. I still pay taxes and sign legal stuff with the Logan name. That's one good thing I got out of the Family—a legal name."

Wagner started on the second half of the massive sub. "You know," he said through the food, "I feel guilty about not giving you more money for the Pier. You're giving me a better operation than I sold you."

"I know. I didn't sell out entirely, remember. I still got half interest."

"Which you split with that kid, Jon, right?"

"Right. And the money you're going to be paying me monthly is sent in two checks, one for me, one for him."

"You see much of him lately?"

"No."

"So what's he doing? Where is he?"

"Playing with a rock 'n' roll band, of all things."

Wagner shook his head. "A nice kid, messed up in a business like that."

Nolan smiled, sipped his beer. "Yeah. When he could've stayed in heisting."

They finished their meal and walked out onto the street. "We still got work to do," Wagner said, hands in pockets, rocking back and forth on his feet. "The accountant'll be down at the Pier by now."

"Let's get it over with," Nolan said.

"You in a hurry or something?"

"Look who's talking."

"Then you'll stay the evening? The Al Pierson Dance Band's playing."

"Sure. Why not." He hadn't given Sherry a definite time he'd be back. There was no rush.

They drove down in Nolan's dark blue LTD.

The Pier was a former Elks Lodge, on the banks of the Iowa River, converted into a seafood restaurant. The bottom floor was the Steamboat Lounge; the main floor was the Mark Twain Dining Room; and the upper floor was the Captain's Ballroom. But Nolan and Wagner were headed for the Accountant's Den, which was to say, the office that had been Nolan's and was now Wagner's, where an accountant was waiting to go over the books, before the final changeover in management.

That took several hours, and by that time Nolan and Wagner were ready to eat again, in the dining room, where an illuminated aquarium built into the length of one wall gave a deep-sea effect. Nolan had the house specialty—pond-raised catfish—the one thing about Iowa City he missed.

Then they went upstairs to the ballroom, where the Al Pierson Band was playing. An eight-piece group in powder-blue tuxes, the Pierson Band had a good, solid sound; Nolan was amazed how full so small a brass section could sound.

About eight months ago, it had occurred to Nolan that in a town full of country-rock discos and live rock 'n' roll clubs, there was nothing for people of *his* generation—the sort of people who flocked to Iowa City for football and basketball weekends. He began providing Saturday night entertainment and soon added Friday, with groups like the Pierson Band. And it went over big—big enough to hire some top names; even the current Glenn Miller configuration had played at the Pier.

"How can you *stand* that shit?" Jon had demanded.

"What shit?"

"That . . . that *Muzak!*"

"You don't know what you're talking about, kid."

"It's worse than fucking *disco!'*

"I considered a disco, but that fad seems pretty dead to me. Besides, I'm not after the college crowd."

"Nolan, I got a piece of this place. What if I want to book a *rock* act in the ballroom?"

"No way in hell. You want the Ramones playing upstairs,

while my businessmen and professors eat surf-and-turf downstairs? Sure."

"Well that music sucks, and that's all there is to it. I knew you were old, but I didn't know you were Lawrence Welk."

And the kid had stalked out.

It was probably the most hostile exchange they'd ever had. Soon Jon was gone, working out of Des Moines with his rock band.

He'd wanted to explain it to Jon. He'd wanted to explain that there were few things in this life that could bring a tear to his eyes, but one of them was Bob Eberley (or a good facsimile) singing "Tangerine." No kid brought up on the Beatles could understand that.

He sat at a side table and had a few drinks and listened to the music and watched the couples dance. The floor was crowded, and most of the people were in their forties, fifties, sixties. Lots of blazers and blue hair. It made him feel old.

He looked at his watch: almost one.

He went to Wagner's office and used the phone to call Sherry. She answered on the fourth ring.

"Hello," her voice said.

"Hi, Sherry. Glad you didn't have the damn answer phone on. I'm sorry I'm so late."

"That's okay."

"I'll be back in a few hours."

"Fine."

"Bye, doll."

"Bye, Logan."

He hung up.

He went back and sat at a table. He ordered another drink. Pierson was playing a Donna Sommer song, and Wagner was out there shaking his bootie with some faded homecoming queen. Then the band began "Just the Way You Are," and Wagner came over, sweating, smiling, and sat with Nolan.

"Still determined to kill yourself, Wag?"

"I guess," Wagner grinned.

"Fuck!" Nolan said.

"What?"

He stood. "Logan she called me."

"Huh?"

"She called me Logan."

"What are you . . ."

"Someone's there with her. The girl's in trouble."

Wagner was saying something, asking him something, but he didn't stop to answer.

7

THE FIRST THING Sherry thought about when she got back to the house was putting out the dog. She'd been gone all day — shopping at both North and South Park with Sara, then sharing a pizza and a movie with her new friend (Sara worked at Nolan's, too, as a waitress). But she knew the dog wouldn't have made a mess. It was completely housebroken. Any dog that dared live with Nolan would have to be housebroken.

She pulled her little Datsun into the drive, parked it off to the side, leaving the way clear to the garage for Nolan when he got back. It was a chilly night, and she felt it: she was wearing the London Fog raincoat Nolan had bought her (it had looked overcast when she left the house that morning) and had as yet to hit him up for a winter coat.

She smiled to herself. Hours of shopping, and all she'd bought was one thing (some designer jeans, the ones Debbie Harry pushed on TV). Being a kept woman of a guy as tight as Nolan did have its drawbacks. Oh, he always came around, eventually; but being a Depression kid, he seemed to have trouble spending the kind of money it took to live in an inflated economy. But she wasn't complaining.

She went in the front door, opened the closet, and turned off the burglar alarm. The alarm was not connected to the local police station (Nolan was respectable these days, but not *that* respectable); it was just something that made enough noise to presumably scare burglars away and perhaps rouse some neighbors.

Actually, Nolan's house was about as isolated as a home in the midst of a housing development could be. Of course, it was a small, exclusive development, of $150,000-and-up homes, of which Nolan's was easily the nicest and most secluded. The rest of the development took up one short street, which turned circular at its dead end and led back out again. Nolan's private drive was just to the right as you entered the street, and the sprawling, ranch-style home was surrounded by trees, the backyard dipping down to expose the lower story, which led out to a patio surrounded by more trees—two acres of them—with just enough yard showing to put a pool. Have to work on that, Sherry thought.

It was a four-bedroom house, two up, two down, with a spacious living room with a wall of picture windows looking out on the trees in back of the house. There were no paintings or other wall decorations to speak of, giving the place a blank look. There was one paneled wall, with fireplace, adjacent to the picture windows. The ceiling was slanted, open-beamed. It was a room of creams and soft browns, like the comfy brown modular couch that faced the TV and stereo area, the TV a 26-inch Sony, the stereo a component number on a rack, with records below—hers on one shelf (running to Barbra Streisand) and his on another (running to Harry James).

She hung up her raincoat and stretched. She was wearing a cream silk blouse and tailored brown wool slacks, very chic, but she'd been wearing them all day, and they were on the verge of rank. She'd kill for a shower.

But first, the dog.

It had not greeted her at the door. Had Nolan been there, and had she come in the door, the dog would have been yapping hysterically, jumping up on her, pushing at her thighs, then nipping her heels. Had she been a stranger, it would have attacked. But she'd come to know that the dog recognized her, by sound, smell, whatever, and when she came in without Nolan, the dog kept its place by the glass doors on the lower, basement floor.

That was because Nolan always entered that way. He never came in through the garage, even though he parked his car there and that would be the easiest way. He never came in through the front door. He always walked past the house down the stone steps into the backyard and unlocked the glass patio doors and came in that way. Because even at this "respectable" time of his life, Sherry had come to learn, Nolan retained an outlaw's paranoia. And entering his home the least expected way (actually, coming down the chimney or through a window would be even less expected, but . . .) seemed par for Nolan's course.

And there the dog was, curled near the glass doors on its circular rug, where it had been sleeping, looking up at her with bright eyes, tail wagging, a white-spotted black terrier about the size of a healthy rabbit.

She leaned down and petted it—got licked for her trouble—and unlocked the glass door and slid it open for the dog to go out. No need to chain it up: it wouldn't go far from where Nolan lived. It wouldn't go out of the yard, in fact.

The dog, like Clint Eastwood in an Italian western, had no name. Nolan referred to it only as "the dog" or "the mutt." It still seemed odd to her that Nolan would have a pet at all. She seldom saw him give the animal affection or attention, but it was clear the dog lived for Nolan's occasional pat.

It had taken her the best part of her entire first week back with him to worm the story out of him. Seemed the mutt had turned up at his back door, half dead; it had been in a bad dog fight or two, had half an ear chewed off, and hadn't eaten for days. "A skeleton with a tail," Nolan had described it.

Apparently the dog had touched a nerve in Nolan that Sherry hadn't known existed. He took the dog in; in fact, he took the dog to a vet—spent money on it! And, while saying Nolan nursed the dog back to health would be going too far, the dog had somehow survived. And somehow knew Nolan was responsible.

If Nolan sat in his reclining chair, reading a paper, watching TV, the dog slept on the floor near his feet. When Nolan slept, the dog slept under the bed. When Nolan ate, the dog sat politely nearby, waiting for the inevitable scraps. Every now and then, Nolan allowed the dog up on his lap; he'd pet it, grant it a smile, and it would curl up and sleep there. But only now and then.

Sherry was more openly affectionate to the dog, and the dog returned the affection; but it loved Nolan. It was, after all, a bitch.

She let the dog in, and it followed her upstairs, tagging after her as she undressed. Then she heard its claws clicking on the stairs, heading back down to wait for Nolan again, as she got in the shower and let the hot needles wash away the hard-earned sweat from a day of shopping centers, pizza, and Robert Redford.

Soon she was in a black Frederick's nightie, sitting on the couch, waiting for Nolan to come home and fuck her. She knew it sounded harsh, but that was what she was in the mood for: a good, hard, horny fuck. And she'd bet that Nolan would feel the same.

She was twenty and had a nice, if not busty, figure; she knew that her appeal to him was her youth, the suppleness of her body, the cuteness of her features, her California blonde hair (dyed or not). And she knew that his appeal to her (beyond this house and his affluence) was as a father figure. A coldly handsome, closed-mouthed father figure, perhaps; a father figure with bullet scars on his muscular body. A father figure who was great in the sack. But a father figure.

She'd first met Nolan at the Tropical, a motel he was running for the Chicago Family. Initially, she'd been a waitress there, and a bad one: it was when she got called on the carpet for spilling food in customers' laps that she ended up in Nolan's lap, and that pretty much was where she'd stayed the rest of that summer.

Then her father had called and told her her mother had had a stroke, and it was back to Ohio for Sherry. There would be no time to finish up college (she had a two-year community college degree and had hoped to get a four-year business degree) and the only job she could find was waitressing at a Denny's. Which was better than hell, but just barely. And when she wasn't waitressing at Denny's, she was looking after her mother, which she didn't mind, because she loved her mother, but it was sad. So very sad.

Three months ago her mother had died.

Sherry started back to college, and only a month in, she knew she couldn't hack it. It wasn't that she was stupid; she wasn't particularly smart, either, but it wasn't that she was stupid. More like bored. She was more bored than waitressing at Denny's. It was a rare week that she didn't think about her summer with Nolan. She had even cried herself to sleep a couple times, missing him, wishing she could have stayed with him.

Then, last month, he called. She didn't even know how he'd managed to track her down, but he had. And he wanted her to come live with him.

"I need a hostess at my new restaurant," he said.

"That's like a waitress, right?"

"Right. Only you don't spill shit on people."

"But Logan, that's my speciality."

"I know. And can the Logan stuff."

Logan was the name she'd known Nolan by at the Tropical.

"How come?"

"I'm using Nolan here. So don't call me Logan anymore. It'll just confuse people."

"Well, I'm already confused."

"That's how I like you."

"I'm also broke."

"I'll send plane fare."

"I'm on my way, then."

Their month together had been a lot of fun, if not a honeymoon. Nolan wasn't altogether humorless, though when he did make a joke, it was so dry, you could miss it if you weren't looking. They made good love together. They got along. He didn't insist that she cook—one thing he wasn't stingy about was taking her out to eat, though he did collect receipts to deduct on the meals on his taxes, claiming he was "checking out my competition." And when she did cook, he didn't complain, even when the results (her Tuna Surprise, for instance) were less than spectacular. Memorable, yes; spectacular, no.

During the first week, the Nolan/Logan thing had been a running gag with them; she'd kept right on calling him Logan, till he finally threatened to turn her over his knee and spank her. She dropped her drawers and said go right ahead. And he had, and more.

But afterward he said, "Seriously—get used to calling me Nolan. I got to stick by one name in one place."

And from then on it was strictly Nolan.

She was watching a "Mission: Impossible" rerun when she remembered the answer phone: she hadn't checked for messages. She went into the kitchen, and the red light was flashing on the little tape unit by the phone on the counter. She rewound the tape and played it back.

"Nolan, this is Jon. I'm calling from a place called the Barn, just this side of Burlington. I'm here with my band."

Jon. That was the kid Nolan was always mentioning. The one who was his partner or something, back when Nolan *wasn't* respectable. She'd never met Jon, but she knew he was someone important in Nolan's life.

"This is going to sound crazy," the voice was saying, sounding tinny coming out of the small speaker, "but I think I saw that bitch Julie. No, scratch that: I *did* see her, no mistaking it. She is *not* dead, Nolan."

What was this about? The kid sounded scared.

"Now the worse news: she saw me. Nolan, if she's been playing dead, she's not going to be happy I found out she's alive.

She's going to cause trouble. So what I'm going to do is finish out the night—it's just before midnight, as I'm talking—and I'm going to confront her, if I can get the chance, and cool this down."

Very nervous, Sherry thought—even desperate.

"In the meantime, if you get home by, oh, twelve-thirty, get in your car and drive down here. Come via 61 all the way, so that if for some reason I end up coming after you, I'll spot you on the highway. It should take you about an hour and forty-five minutes to two hours to get here; the band quits at one-thirty, the club stays open till two, and then it's another half-hour or forty-five minutes of tearing down equipment and loading. Which means there'll be too many people around for her to try anything till three, I'd say. Or anyway, two-thirty. So if you can leave there by twelve-thirty, get down here. Otherwise, stay put and wait for me to get back to you."

It was a disturbing message. She didn't understand it, but that only made it all the more disturbing; she rewound it, listened to it again, then rewound it again so that Nolan could hear it when he got home.

But one thing was certain: the twelve-thirty deadline was past; it was quarter till one now.

She went back to the TV, found an old crime movie with Cornell Wilde, which she started to watch, then switched to "Second City TV." The crime movie was hitting just a little too close to home.

It took only about four minutes of "Second City" to get her laughing; she hadn't forgotten the disturbing answer-phone message, but it wasn't dominating her thoughts now. But she did wonder when Nolan would get here.

That thought had barely flicked through her mind when she heard the footsteps on the stairs and smiled. God, he was quiet coming in. Nobody was that quiet Usually, the dog would have yapped at him, though, happy to see him. Not tonight. That was odd.

Still on the couch, she turned her head and glanced back at Nolan.

Only it wasn't Nolan.

It was two men: one of them, disturbingly, looked a little like Nolan, but a younger Nolan, about thirty-five, with no mustache and short, curly, permed hair that gave him a Caesar sort of look. He was in black—black slacks, black turtleneck, black gloves. The other man was coming up the stairs behind the Nolan clone, in shadows; she couldn't see him yet.

She reached for a heavy sculpted glass paperweight on the coffee table near the couch.

It exploded before she could touch it, shards of glass nicking at her arm. Choking back a scream, she clutched her blood-flecked arm with her other hand and glanced back at the men. The Caesar type had an automatic in his hand; there was an attachment on the end of it—a silencer?—and smoke was curling out the barrel. He was smiling faintly.

"I don't like shooting at Art Deco pieces," the man said. His voice was a smooth, curiously pleasant baritone. "Don't make me shoot any more furniture, dear. I'd sooner shoot you."

She felt very naked in her Frederick's nightie, and flashed onto an absurd thought: *Thank God I didn't go crotchless!*

Then she saw the other man. He, too, looked familiar. Then she placed him: he was a ringer for that guy that used to be on that Angie Dickinson police show. But, again, younger—perhaps thirty. He had curly, permed hair too, and a silly smile that scared her more than the tight, controlled smile of the other man. This one, too, was in black; this one, too, had an automatic with an attachment.

The first man came over to her, with a gloved hand brushed the glass from the coffee table, and sat down, the gun casual in his hand, but pointing at her. He was tanned. Handsome, in an unsettling way.

"Where's Logan?" He said.

"Logan?" she said.

"Or Nolan. Whatever he's calling himself here."

"He lives here," she said. Stupidly, she thought.

"We *know*," the other's voice said. She sat up, so she could see the other man. He was over turning off the TV, then crouching to look through the albums under the stereo. Looking through the records. Jesus. What kind of . . .

"Sally," the second guy said, holding up an album. "She's got Barry Manilow." Then to her: "You got good taste lady. How about Rupert Holmes? You got Rupert Holmes?"

"Uh, no," she said. *What the fuck . . .*

"Put some records on, Infante," the first one, Sally, said. "Put on the live Manilow album."

"That thing where he does the medley of commercials kills me," Infante said. He had the slightest speech impediment: Elmer Fudd after therapy.

"Does it kill you?" Sally asked her, smiling, apparently amused by his flaky partner.

"I hope not," Sherry said.

"So do I," Sally said. "I don't like killing things, but I will if I have to. So will Infante, won't you, Infante? It was Infante killed the dog. I didn't have the heart to."

She brought her hand up to her face, bit her knuckles. She tried to hold back the tears, the trembling. It was no use. Barry Manilow was singing, "Even now . . ."

"Go ahead and cry, dear. Infante!"

Infante was right there, like a fast cut in a movie. "Yeah, Sally?"

"Check out the house. This Logan or whoever isn't here, but check out the lay of the land, and then get the lady some Kleenex. Her makeup's starting to run."

"Sure, Sally."

And Infante was gone.

Sally smiled; that the face was vaguely like Nolan's did nothing to reassure her—if anything, it only terrified her more. She had never been so scared; she'd never been so conscious of her heart, pounding in her chest, as if trying to get out.

Sally touched her arm; his touch was cold as a snake.

"If you rape me," she said, tightly, teeth clenched, "Nolan'll kill you."

Sally laughed; it was almost a gentle laugh. He patted her arm. "We're not going to rape you." Then Infante was there, holding the Kleenex out to Sally, who took it and passed it on to Sherry. "We're not going to rape her, are we, Infante?"

Infante looked at Sherry as though she was a slug. "Are you kidding?"

Sally held Sherry's hand; in the background Barry Manilow sang. Sally said, "All we want to know is where Nolan is."

Sherry said nothing.

"Is he coming back soon?"

Sherry said nothing.

"He's out of town, isn't he?"

Sherry said nothing.

Sally said, "Flick your Bic, would you, Infante?"

"Sure," Infante said. He got his lighter out. Sally held both of Sherry's arms down while Infante grasped both of her feet around the ankles and locked them in the crook of one arm as he held the lighter's flame to the bottom of her right foot, just under the toes.

She screamed. The pain was intense; it went on forever.

"Three seconds," Sally said to her. "You want to try for ten?"

"Please . . ."

"I don't get pleasure from this. Infante doesn't get pleasure from this. Do you, Infante?"

Infante, still gripping her ankles, grinned and said, "No."

"If we were sadists," Sally said, leaning in close, "we'd burn your face, not the bottom of your feet." He blew against her cheek; his breath was minty.

"There's nothing I can tell you," she managed.

"Infante. Flick your Bic."

"No!"

"Wait a second, Infante."

Barry Manilow was singing about the Copa; Infante was singing along, softly.

"Well?" Sally said to her.

"He didn't tell me where he was going. He just said he'd be gone most of the day, on business."

"Flick your Bic, Infante."

"That's the truth!"

The other foot, this time; the pain was searing, like a branding iron, lasting for days.

"Five seconds, that time," Sally said. "You want to get serious, dear? Or you'll never dance again."

Infante snickered at that, still singing to himself.

"I'm telling the truth!" she said.

Sally thought about that.

"Please," she said, "he didn't tell me, he didn't tell me, why should he bother telling me?"

"When will he be home?"

"I thought he'd be back by now. He said about midnight."

Sally let go of her arms, looked at his watch. "Jesus," he said to himself.

"Maybe she's telling the truth, Sally," Infante said, still gripping her ankles, the lighter in hand.

"Maybe. I wouldn't want him coming in on this, that's for sure."

The phone rang.

Sally looked at her sharply. "Could that be him?"

She nodded.

"Where's the phone?"

Another ring.

"In the kitchen," she said.

Infante said, "Extension's in the bedroom," releasing her ankles and running to the bedroom.

"Pick it up on the fourth ring!" Sally called out.

He was dragging her to the kitchen; she felt the skin on her burned feet catching and tearing against the carpet.

He pushed her toward the phone, and she picked it up on the fourth ring.

It was Nolan.

She answered his questions, Sally's automatic with its attachment kissing her neck.

Got to warn him, give him a sign, she thought.

"I'll be back in a few hours," he was saying.

"Fine," she heard herself say.

"Bye, doll."

"Bye, Logan."

She hung up.

Would he pick up on it? That she'd called him Logan? Had that been warning enough?

In the other room, Barry Manilow was singing, "This Time We Made It."

Sally dragged her back to the couch and she passed out.

8

NOLAN LEFT his LTD on the street, a block away, and made his way up behind the house, through the sloping woods. He stayed within the trees, not going across the lawn until he was parallel to the corner of the house—some lights on, upstairs—and then, keeping low, made for the sliding glass doors off the patio.

It had taken him just under an hour-and-a-half to get here; he'd come via Interstate 80, and no Highway Patrol had stopped him despite his speeding. He was grateful for that much. Whoever had Sherry in the house wouldn't expect him back this soon. He was grateful for that, too. But he wished he had a gun.

Somebody inside the house had a gun. He saw the concave pucker in the glass where the bullet had gone through. Beyond it he saw the slumped form of his small dog. The door's lock had been jimmied, so he didn't bother with his key. He just slid it carefully open. And stepped inside.

No lights on down here. But his night vision was in full force, and moonlight came in the doors behind him, and he could see the big open room, which would be a game room when he got around to putting a pool table in. There was a fireplace, as there was upstairs, but no furniture yet. Nowhere to hide, unless it was in one of the rooms off the hallway directly across from him:

the two guest bedrooms, extra john, furnace room. He stood silently for a good minute. He heard muffled sounds upstairs. Nothing down here.

He slid the door shut behind him.

He knelt and gave his dog a pat.

He didn't have a gun. He didn't have a goddamn gun. He'd been in such a goddamn hurry to get here, he hadn't even stopped to ask Wagner for something. And he didn't have anything stashed down here, no weapon of any kind. He always went to the precaution of coming in the back way, but he hadn't bothered with stashing a gun. Stupid. He looked at the boxes stacked over against one wall. What was in those? Anything useful?

Still kneeling, he smiled to himself. Patted the dog's warm body. Got some blood on his hand but didn't wipe it off.

Some of that stuff in the boxes was Sherry's. She'd told her father she was getting an apartment when she moved here, so he'd given her some things: pots, pans, and so on. Also silverware.

He slipped out of his shoes and moved soundlessly across the carpeted floor to the boxes. Very carefully he sorted through the first box; the wooden case with silverware in it was under some Tupperware. He removed one stainless steel steak knife with a four-inch blade. He held it tight in a fist wet with the animal's blood.

There was only one way up, and that was the stairs, coming right up into the living room, at the back. Half a flight, a landing, then, to the left, another half a flight, and bam. If they were waiting for him, watching for him, he was dead. If they weren't, he had a chance. The stairs were carpeted, and he was quiet. He went up the first half-flight and waited, just one step below the landing. Listened.

Music.

"I think she's coming around, Sally," a voice said. An immature voice.

"Doesn't matter," another, older voice said. "She doesn't know anything else we want to know."

"Maybe we should ask her how he comes in. There's more than one way in."

"You may have a point."

"You want me to hold her feet again?"

"I don't think that'll be necessary."

Music—they were playing music on the goddamn stereo. Barry Manilow, wasn't it? Crazy.

"She's awake, Sally."

That name Sally, again. A man named Sally. Sal. Sal and Infante. The two bodyguards working for Hines, the local Family man.

"Which way does he come in?" he heard Sal asking.

"Front door," Sherry's voice said. Hurting.

"Maybe you better hold her feet again, Infante."

"No!" Sherry said. "It's the garage way. Doorway's in the hall."

"You telling the truth? Hold her feet, Infante."

"It's the truth!" Sherry all but screamed.

Actually, Nolan would have preferred Sherry really tell the truth. That would send at least one of them down here. Well, maybe there was a way. . . .

He stepped onto the landing. Looked up the stairs. No one at the top. There appeared to be only the two men here with Sherry, and they were in another part of the living room above.

He went up a few steps. Peeked over the edge of what was the living room floor, at left, through the black latticework railing.

Sherry was on the couch.

Infante's back was to Nolan, and the guy was apparently holding Sherry by the ankles. The other one, Sally, was pinning down her arms, questioning her, his back partially to Nolan.

"Better flick your Bic, Infante," Sally was saying. "Don't burn the same spot."

Nolan's hand tightened on the steak knife as the pain made Shery jerk up, into a sitting position, while Sally covered her mouth with a hand to stifle her scream.

But when Sherry jerked up, her pain-widened eyes met Nolan's. He was visible from the shoulders up. He gestured: raised a finger and pointed downward, thinking *Send them to me, doll. Send them to me.*

Then he ducked down out of sight. Sat on the steps.

"All right!" Sherry said. "All right. It isn't the front door. It isn't the garage way, either."

"What way is it dear?" Sally said.

Nolan slipped back down the stairs.

"He comes in the way you did," she said.

"The basement!" Infante said.

Brilliant Nolan thought. He was standing with his back to the wall, just at the bottom of the stairs, to the right.

"I better move that dog," Sally said. "Shit! And he'll see the bullet hole, too. Damn!"

"What'll we do, Sally?"

"Shut off the fuckin' music, for one thing. He could be here in fifteen, twenty minutes. Christ! I'll go down and get rid of the dog."

The music stopped.

Infante said, "He won't notice the bullet hole, or that we broke in through there, till he gets up close."

"Yeah, you're right. So if I'm watching for him down there, I can nail him right through the glass door while he's standing out in the yard. Yeah. Okay. You stick with the bitch here, in case he varies from pattern and comes in up here."

"Okay, Sally."

"Just shoot him. Don't talk to him."

"Yes, Sally. Sally."

"Yeah?"

"You be careful I wouldn't want nothing to happen to you."

There was a pause.

Then Sally said, "Yeah. You, too."

Nolan heard Sally on the stairs. He stepped off the last step, and Nolan put a hand over his mouth and the steak knife in his back, lower right.

Nolan eased him to the floor. Sally gurgled and died, getting blood on Nolan's hand. Nolan wiped his hand on Sally's shirt. Then he took the man's silenced 9 mm from a limp hand and left him there, the knife handle sticking out of his back like something to pick him up by.

Nolan went slowly back up the stairs, gun in hand.

Infante was sitting on the arm of the couch, his back to Nolan, blocking Nolan's view of Sherry, who was still lying there. He couldn't risk a shot, for fear of hitting her. He should probably try to lure Infante downstairs . . . but Infante would likely drag Sherry along, not wanting to leave her unattended, so that was out.

Nothing to do but try to come up behind him slow.

Nolan was halfway between the top of the stairs and the couch when Infante turned and with a startled expression that was only vaguely human, shot at Nolan three times with the silenced 9 mm's twin. Nolan dove for the floor and rolled into the entryway area by the front door while a plaster wall took the bullets, spitting dust.

The kitchen was off the entryway, and Nolan ducked in there, as it connected to the living room and would allow him to enter on the opposite side, which should confuse Infante and give Nolan a better look at where Sherry was, to take a shot at Infante and still keep Sherry out of harm's way.

And Sherry was on the couch, all right, but Infante was heading down the stairs, into the basement, shouting, "Sally! Sally!"

Nolan went to Sherry, who reached for him, hugged him.

"Are you okay, doll?"

She was smiling, crying. "My feet are killing me."

"I better go after him."

"No! Stay with me."

There was an anguished cry from downstairs—a wail.

"I'll kill you!" Infante's voice, muffled but distinct, came from below.

"Maybe he'll come up after me," Nolan said.

But the next sound from below was the glass doors sliding/slamming shut.

Nolan ran to the picture windows. He saw Infante scurrying across the yard, off to the right, into the woods.

"Stay put," Nolan told Sherry.

"Nolan . . ."

"Stay put!"

"Where would I go?" she yelled at him, angry for a moment.

Nolan went out the front door, fanning the gun around in front of him. The full moon was keeping everything well lit; there was a pale, eerie wash on the world. But no sign of Infante.

Then he heard an engine start, a car squeal away.

He stood there a moment and let the cool air cool him down.

Then he went back in. To Sherry.

He examined her feet.

"Sons of bitches," he said.

"They hurt. They really hurt."

"Second-degree burns. You're lucky."

"Oh, yeah. Lucky."

"They've started to blister. Third degree would've been trouble. I'm going to get you some cold water to soak them in."

"Please."

He got a pan with ice and water in it and eased her to a sitting position, and she slid her feet in, making a few intake-of-breath sounds, but seeming to like it, once done.

"I should get you to a hospital," he said. "I should get you to an emergency room."

"How can you do that?" she said. "They'll want to know how it happened. I don't know what this is about, but I know you. And I know this isn't something you'll want the police or anybody in on."

He scratched his head and said, "Right. Burns on the feet are dangerous, though. You need a doctor."

"Sara's boyfriend is a doctor."

"Sara? At the club?"

"Right."

"Will he keep his mouth shut? Will he make a post-midnight house call?"

"He's a married doctor. He'll do anything Sara asks him."

"Good. What's Sara's number?"

"It's in the back of the phonebook."

"I want you to stay with her for a few days."

"Where will you be?"

"I don't know yet. I don't know what this is about, either."

He got up to go to the kitchen to call Sara.

"Did you know those two men?" Sherry asked.

He turned and looked at her. For all she'd been through, she looked terrific, sitting there in a short black nightie, soaking her feet.

"Yeah," he said. "A couple of guys who work for Hines."

"Hines. Isn't he connected?"

"Yeah, Hines is Family. That bothers me. I haven't had any Family trouble for a long time."

"You going to talk to Hines?"

"He's out of town. And anyway, those two were Family, out of Chicago, before they got assigned to Hines. They could've got their orders from somebody other than Hines. With Hines out of town, that almost seems likely."

"You've got Family friends."

"There's Felix, that lawyer I always dealt with. But if I call him, he'll lie to me, if I'm on the shit list again. I don't know. I think I'm going to have to go out and knock heads together and see what's going on."

He went to the kitchen.

"Nolan!" she called out

He came back out and said. "What?"

"I almost forgot. There's a message for you on the answer machine. A long one."

"Oh?"

"It's from that friend of yours."

"Jon?"

"Yes. It sounded like he was in trouble. Maybe this has something to do with that."

But before she had finished her sentence, Nolan was in the kitchen playing the message. He listened to it twice.

He came back talking to himself, saying, "Julie, alive? If so, how is she connected to anybody Family? I don't get it." Then, to Sherry: "Did those guys hear that message? Did they get that out of you?"

"No," she said. "I kept thinking they'd want to know, if they'd known to ask. But they didn't ask, and I was happy to keep it from them."

"Good girl."

"You missed your deadline, you know. You were supposed to go after your friend if you got home by twelve-thirty."

"Well, I didn't. And he isn't here yet, so I'm going after him anyway. It's my only lead."

"Did you call Sara?"

"Not yet. Listen. Tell her nothing. Nothing about how you got the burns. Nothing about the shooting. I'll let her know I'll make it right by her, for helping, no questions asked. Then I'll have to bandage your feet up, best I can, till her doctor friend can apply proper dressings at her place."

"Okay."

"Then I got to bury something in the woods, and I'm off."

"You mean that guy downstairs? Sally? You killed him?"

"Yeah, I killed him. But I don't mean him. I'll dump him someplace. He doesn't rate a burial. I'm talking about my dog."

3

9

JON CAME TO.

He knew three things immediately: he was in the back seat of a car, on his side; it was dark, so it wasn't morning yet, or anyway the sun wasn't up; and his head ached so bad, his eyes hurt.

He sat up; it took some doing, but he sat up. His hands were behind him, and he could feel the cold steel of handcuffs; his legs were bound at the ankles with thick, heavily knotted rope, like the handiwork of a very ambitious, sadistic Boy Scout.

Or Girl Scout.

He looked out the window to the left. The dyke, Ron, black leather jacket, ducktail, and all, was standing in an arrogant slouch, listening to Julie talk.

Julie.

She was still wearing the white outfit, but the tinted glasses were gone, an affectation she presumably dropped during more private moments. She was gesturing as she spoke, and occasionally she would reach out and touch Ron's face, casually.

The two of them were standing in the midst of a big open graveled area, a parking lot. This car Jon was in the back of was one of only two cars parked in it The other one was a low-slung sportscar, a Porsche, Jon thought, the color of which he couldn't make out—something light pastel—and the owner *had* to be Julie.

Behind them was a building that appeared to be an old brick warehouse, but there was a neon sign, which wasn't on, over a covered entryway, indicating it had been converted into something else. A restaurant or a club, maybe. He couldn't tell, exactly; he couldn't really see that well.

He tried to make out what they were saying, but it was muffled; they were a good twenty feet away. He pressed his ear to the glass of the car window and listened. He began to pick up some of the conversation.

"Just hold onto him for me," Julie was saying.

"You want him to disappear forever, he can," the dyke said.

"Not yet. In a day or two, maybe."

"It don't matter to me. I'd soon cut his throat as look at him."

A sick feeling swept over Jon—not nausea: hopelessness. A physical sense of hopelessness.

Then he didn't hear anything. He took his ear away from the glass and looked out the window, and Julie and the dyke were kissing. There was a full moon tonight, but it didn't lend much romance to the scene, the way Jon saw it.

Then the big sandy-haired guy with glasses, the Incredible Hulk guy, came out of the warehouse, and Julie and Ron broke it up; Julie walked to meet the guy, and the dyke just stood there, hands on her butt, looking sullen. Julie and the guy talked for what seemed forever and was maybe five minutes.

How the fuck could she be *alive*, anyway?

He and Nolan had driven to Ft. Madison and seen the twisted, burnt wreckage of the car she'd been in. Or was supposed to have been in. Didn't make sense.

But what did make sense, where Julie was concerned? The only thing you could count on was she'd use her looks to manipulate those around her. Like she had with that poor dead bastard Rigley, the Port City bank president.

She'd put him up to it They didn't know it at first but it became obvious as soon as she came into it. Rigley could never have done it on his own.

Rigley had come into the Pier, about a year ago, and announced to Nolan that he recognized him as one of the men who had held his bank up two years before. Rigley then blackmailed Nolan, and Jon, into helping him rob his own bank, to cover up an embezzlement The robbery had gone off without a hitch, but when it came to making the split at Rigley's cottage on the Cedar River, he and his beautician girlfriend, Julie, put a double-cross in motion.

But at the last minute, the banker panicked, and when Julie fired a shotgun meant for Nolan, Rigley got in front of the blast. Nolan dove for the girl, but she swung the now-empty shotgun around and whacked him in the head, and he went down.

Jon was under the dead banker. He pushed the corpse off and grabbed for the girl's arm as she fled, but she caught him in the gut with the gunstock, and then again on the back of the neck, when he doubled over.

Moments later he came to, grabbed his .38 from off the floor, and went out after her.

Julie was in her yellow Mustang, the laundry bag of money sitting in back like a person.

He had her in his sights, but he couldn't do it. He couldn't shoot. Couldn't kill her.

So he shot at her tires; maybe hit one.

Then she was gone.

And minutes later he and Nolan were pursuing her. There were only two ways she could go: back to Port City, which on the heels of the bank robbery was unlikely, or toward West Liberty, a little town near where she'd lived before moving into Rigley's cottage.

On the outskirts of West Liberty, they saw it: the Mustang, with a flat tire, pulled over on the shoulder.

In front of it was a blue Ford that said WEST LIBERTY SHERIFF'S DEPT. on the side. Julie was in the back seat of the Ford. So was the sack of money.

The sheriff or deputy or whatever, a pudgy-faced guy with a weak chin, close-set eyes, five o'clock shadow, and a western-style hat, sat in front, getting ready to pull out on the highway, into town. He apparently had stopped Julie for driving recklessly in a car with a flat tire, and stumbled onto something a bit bigger.

Julie saw Nolan and Jon as they drove by, but didn't alert the sheriff. Nolan and Jon drove back to Iowa City to sit it out.

That night, back at the antique shop, in the upstairs living quarters, they kept the radio on and the TV too, waiting for news of the West Liberty arrest. It never came.

"I think we been snookered," Nolan said. "I think that West Liberty hick was in on it with her."

"Nolan, that's nuts," Jon had said. "She couldn't've planned ahead for a flat tire. She couldn't've put something that complex together."

"Yeah," he said. "You're right."

"So now what?"

"We keep waiting."

The next morning it was on the news: on a narrow bridge on the highway outside Ft. Madison, a gas tanker truck struck a car, head on. There had been an explosion. The two men in the truck were killed, as was the woman driving the car. Several thousand dollars in burnt bills in Port City bank wrappers linked the young woman driving the car to yesterday's Port City bank robbery. In the days to come, the woman, though burned beyond recognition, was identified as the dead bank president's mistress. The cops put a scenario together for the robbery and its aftermath that did not, thankfully, include Nolan and Jon.

But Nolan had not been satisfied. He went to Ft. Madison and looked at the burnt wreckage of the Mustang.

"I think we been snookered," he said again.

Again, Jon said, "You're nuts. She was running, and it all caught up with her."

"You mean God killed her?"

"Well . . ."

"He doesn't have that good a sense of humor."

There was one thing Nolan could still do, and Jon drove him, after a good month had passed, to West Liberty. The weak-chinned deputy sheriff—whose name was Creel—lived in a little white frame house a few blocks from the outskirts of town—a few blocks from where he stopped Julie's Mustang. So at two in the morning one night, with Jon at his side, Nolan knocked on Creel's door.

Creel answered in his pajamas. Nolan, wearing a ski mask, put a gun in Creel's neck.

Within the house, a female voice from upstairs called, "Honey? Is something wrong?"

Nolan said softly, "Nothing's wrong."

Creel looked at Nolan wide-eyed, slack-jawed; he looked at Jon standing just behind Nolan, also in a ski mask, also with a gun.

"Nothing's wrong, honey," Creel called back. "Just some sheriffing!"

And Nolan walked the deputy around back and had him sit in a swing on a swing set. Creel had kids, apparently.

"Tell me about Julie," Nolan said.

"What?"

"Tell me why you didn't turn Julie and that money in last month."

And Creel did something amazing: he started to cry. He sat in the swing and cried.

Then he talked.

"I was nuts about that cunt. She had a beauty shop in town. For two years I tried to make her. I usually don't cheat around, but that cunt was s-o-o-o-o-o-o beautiful. And she laughed at me when I came onto her. *Two years* I tried making her."

"Get to the point."

"There's not much to tell. I saw this car driving wild. Flat tire. Pulled it over and it was this Julie. She had a shotgun, but it was empty. And she had a bag of money. All that fuckin' money. She said, 'You hear about the Port City bank job this afternoon?' I said yeah. She said, 'This is the money. Hundreds of thousands here. Nobody knows I got it but you.' Jesus, I said. She says, 'You want to be rich and fuck me whenever you want?' I didn't say nothin'. She says, 'Rich,' and reaches for my dick. 'Nobody's home at my place,' I says. My wife and the kids was at her mom's in Des Moines, for Christmas. She says, 'Drive us there, then. Now.' And I did."

Creel started laughing.

"We parked the Mustang in back here, in the garage, and took the bag of money in and plopped it on the kitchen table. She and I sat and played with the money and laughed. Then we went upstairs to the bedroom and, sweet Jesus, I fucked her. Three times, and it was . . . nothing like it, ever. We was in bed together, and I drifted off to sleep, thinking it was a dream, a crazy dream. I woke up a couple hours later, handcuffed to the bed. Alone in the house."

Creel sat there, swinging.

"You believe she's dead?" Nolan asked.

"If she isn't, I'd like to kill her." He laughed. "Or fuck her." Then he just sat there blankly. Swinging.

"We never had this conversation," Nolan said.

"Right," Creel said.

And Nolan and Jon went back to Iowa City and forgot about it.

Now, a year later, Jon was in the back seat of a car, handcuffed like that dumb asshole Creel, while Julie and some dyke named Ron talked about whether or not to kill him.

Right now Julie was still talking to that sandy-haired guy. If only they'd go into that warehouse for a while, maybe he could *do* something. . . .

The car he was in was an old souped-up Ford, with tuck 'n' roll upholstery, four-on-the-floor, stereo speakers on the back ledge. He was locked in, of course, but maybe . . .

On the other side of the car, the one facing away from Julie and Ron and the Hulk, Jon bit the tip of the locking knob on the door. He pulled up his with teeth. It clicked.

He glanced over to see if the figures out in the parking lot had heard it. It had sounded incredibly loud to him. But they still stood there, Julie and the guy, talking, Ron doing her James Dean slouch.

With his back to the door, he used this cuffed hands to grasp the door handle. He pulled. The latch gave, but he didn't open the door. He was still watching the people in the lot. To see if they'd heard the sound—which seemed to him to echo across the world like a shout in the Grand Canyon. But they didn't seem to. Ron glanced over, but just momentarily.

He waited a minute or so.

Then he pushed the door open a bit, hoping the dome light wouldn't go on. It didn't. One small break. He edged it open and slipped down out of the car onto the gravel and eased the door shut.

On his belly, he looked under the car, toward Julie and the Hulk and Ron. He saw their legs; they hadn't moved.

He looked off, in the opposite direction. Another twenty feet of parking lot, then trees. If he could make it to the trees, and perhaps hide, then eventually work the ropes off his ankles, and find a highway . . .

He crawled on his belly. The gravel was rough; it scraped him. He was only in T-shirt and jeans. His mouth, already tasting like an old gym sock, took in dust.

He could hear them talking. They hadn't noticed him. Trees ahead, a few yards.

Then a voice. Ron's.

"Hey!"

Feet ran on gravel.

He tried to get on his feet; maybe he could hop faster than he could crawl.

He never found out.

A foot was on his back, and then he heard Ron say, "You ain't goin' noplace," and she grabbed him by his bound ankles and dragged him, face down, back to her car.

10

HAROLD TOOK off his glasses and rubbed his eyes. He was sitting behind the metal desk in the small paneled office at the rear of his and Julie's club, the Paddlewheel. He was waiting for the phone to ring.

The Paddlewheel was a big place, an old converted warehouse near the banks of the Mississippi, in Gulf Port, Illinois; it contained a restaurant, several bars, several dance floors with stages, and a casino. But Harold's office was small.

Harold, of course, was big, a big man who felt uncomfortable in his small office, physically uncomfortable, psychologically uncomfortable. This small office was just another unspoken insult in his life with Julie. But he loved her. He loved her. And if she didn't love him back, well, she didn't love anybody else, either. Except Julie, of course.

Julie had a large office upstairs, with a huge wood-topped desk, bulky old-fashioned safe, file cabinets, chairs, bar, television, stereo, a couch where she slept sometimes. Almost an apartment, and she did use it as a place to go, to stay, even overnight—when she wanted to get away from him for a while, Harold knew.

They lived together in a big white house with pillars, a near-mansion built ten years before by a wealthy farmer for a beloved wife who divorced him a year later. The place was several miles outside Gulf Port, in the midst of rich farmland that Julie now owned, one of several investments she'd made with the money they were earning from the Paddlewheel. It was a four-bedroom home that required a housekeeper to come in three times a week, filled with antiques Julie picked up (her only hobby); they slept in separate bedrooms, though he was allowed to join her in her bed for love-making a few times a week.

As for his small office on the basement level, she claimed it was a ploy of sorts; it was obviously necessary to keep considerable cash on hand for the casino and, she said, she wanted a certain amount beyond that in case the day came that they should need to leave in a hurry. So the big old safe in her office, in which a few thousand was kept, was a decoy; the safe containing over $100,000 was in the floor of Harold's small office, a little vault in the corner, under the carpet.

It had been a long and disturbing evening. What it should have been was a pleasant night out—dinner at the Barn, followed by scouting the band there for possible fill-in at the Paddlewheel. But then this Jon kid turned up out of Julie's past.

Julie had taken the money from that bank job and turned it into the Paddlewheel, from which had come land holdings and a sporting goods store in Burlington and . . . and Jon and Logan would want their share, now that they knew she was alive. Julie claimed they'd want even more—revenge, she said. But Harold didn't really buy that. He knew Julie well enough to know that if there was one thing Julie loved besides Julie, it was money; that was the only fever in her, and she wouldn't do the smart thing, the right thing, and call this Logan and the kid Jon in and admit her deceptions and cut them in for a share. No way in hell. She'd do anything but that. Harold knew that only too well. He knew only too well what Julie was capable of, for money.

He sat rubbing his eyes, waiting for the phone to ring. It was almost two in the morning, and he was exhausted. He wanted to go to his room at the house and sleep. Just sleep.

But he had to wait till the phone rang.

Those two guys Julie had contacted, the ones her Chicago connection put her onto, should have called by now.

He didn't like being part of this. He didn't like being any part of killing. It wasn't the first time she'd got him into being part of something that was directly opposed to everything he'd ever been taught, that he'd ever believed in. He didn't understand it, how he could have come to believe in one thing, live for one thing: Julie. The few nights a week in her bed, doled out like a child's allowance; the occasional tender look; those few times a week she'd squeeze his arm and smile, or touch his face. He lived for those. He didn't believe any of them, but he wanted to. And he took what he could get.

And then there were those rare, real moments when she got blue and came to him for some emotional support. When she needed a man to lean on, and for a while, a short while, he'd be a man to her, and to himself.

The phone rang.

It was the long-distance operator with a collect call for anyone from Mr. Smith. Harold accepted the call.

A young, out-of-breath voice said, "This is Infante."

"I was told I'd be speaking to a Sal," Harold said.

"Well, you're speaking to Infante!"

"I better speak to Sal."

"You can't! You can't . . . he's dead. Sally's dead."

Dead. So it was starting, Harold thought. It was starting again.

On the other end of the phone, Infante seemed to be sobbing.

"Are you all right, Infante?"

"I'm fine!" the young voice said with defiance.

"Where are you?"

"Some restaurant I'm at a restaurant. Denny's."

"Where?"

"I don't know. Port City? I'm using a pay phone."

"In a booth?"

"It's a kind of stall."

"Well, keep your voice down, then, Infante."

"Yeah. Okay."

"What happened?"

"We had the guy's girlfriend. We were waiting for him. But he came in and surprised us. He killed Sally. With a knife! With a goddamn knife!"

"Please. Why did you leave the Quad Cities?"

"I couldn't stay! He knows who I am, this Logan or Nolan or whatever. He'd come after me."

"Then you better go someplace where you have friends who can hide you."

"I'm not *hiding* from that son-of-a-bitch! I *want* him. He killed *Sally*! Don't you get it?"

"Look. Infante, is it? Go to your friends—"

"*Sally* was my friend. He was all I had! That fucker Nolan, I'm going to *kill* him!"

You better decide whether you're going to kill him or run from him, Harold thought But he said, "What are your plans, then?"

"I'm coming to you."

"Infante, I wouldn't . . ."

"I don't care what you'd do. I'm coming. You owe me money."

"That'll be taken care of . . ."

"It sure will. And you can put me up somewhere. While we wait."

"Wait for what?"

"For Nolan."

Harold rubbed his eyes again.

"Yes," he said into the phone, "I suppose you're right He will be coming, won't he?"

Harold gave Infante some directions and hung up the phone.

Harold rarely drank. It was a holdover from his football days; he'd taken training very seriously. And he still took vitamins, watched his diet, worked out at a spa. He was into his thirties, and most men of his physical type would have gone to fat by now. Not Harold.

But right now he felt like a drink. He'd have to go out to that parking lot, where Julie was dealing with that crazy lez, and tell her about Infante. Thinking about her with Ron gave him a sick feeling; thinking about what Infante had told him, and how Julie would react to it, made him feel sicker. He went to the bar just outside his office and unlocked the booze and mixed himself a Manhattan.

Despite his not drinking much, he could make a hell of a mixed drink. He'd been a bartender for three years, after all. That's what he'd been doing when Julie came back into his life a century ago. Last year.

Of course he and Julie went back a lot farther than a year ago. She had been the high school cheerleader, the homecoming queen candidate, the local beauty contest winner, who had caught the eye of the local football hero—Harold. His eye wasn't all she'd caught: on the eve of his freshman year at State, she announced she was pregnant.

No problem: he had scholarship money, and an extra job. And he loved her. Very, very much. So they married. They had a beautiful little girl, Lisa. They were happy. Or at least he was. Julie seemed moody, but it wasn't a bad first year for a marriage. Then his grades got bad.

He hadn't been in Vietnam long when he got the "Dear Harold" letter.

He didn't see any action in 'Nam. He'd had two things going for him: bad eyes and the ability to type.

He was a clerk typist, in the rear area, and never heard a shell go off. It was an easy war for Harold.

Peace had been another matter. He was divorced from a woman he still loved. He was a football hero without a college degree and had few qualifications for anything outside of clerical work or a factory job. He ended up a bartender, in an all-night joint in Gulf Port, across the river from Burlington, where he'd gone to work in a college buddy's office as a clerk. He'd thought about bettering himself. He'd considered going back to college and trying again; he'd considered going to a business school, for a two-year degree at least, to bolster his clerical credentials.

But he gave that up after one of the two-week summer visits he had yearly with his daughter. She was being raised by Julie's younger sister and her husband, an executive with a public relations firm in Minneapolis; she was very happy with them. They were her parents, for all intents and purposes. And while

Lisa—who was thirteen now—loved her father, enjoyed their visits together, she made it clear she was happy where she was. And one thing Harold wouldn't do was make his daughter unhappy.

There were only two things Harold wanted in life: his daughter, Lisa, who was lost to him, except in the "Uncle Daddy" sense, and his ex-wife, Julie, who had gone into business, with a beauty shop in a small Iowa town called West Liberty, and who wanted nothing to do with him—though she did call him on the phone now and then, when she was feeling low.

So Harold had settled into life-as-existence. He worked at menial jobs. The bartending gig was about the longest-term employment he'd had since the service. He took an odd pride in his ability to mix a good drink, any drink, and talked sports with customers till all hours. Harold did still get some pleasure out of watching sports on TV. That, and listening to old Beach Boys and Beatles albums from his high school days, was about all Harold had.

Till that afternoon last year when Julie showed up at the bar.

She had looked strange. And beautiful, of course. She was wearing a clingy blood-red sweater and slacks. She had a wild look, her eyes aglitter, her hair slightly disarrayed. An animal look. And there was good reason: she was on the run.

"Do you want me back?" she whispered. Just like that. Leaning across the bar. There were only a few customers in the place. Jody's, like most Gulf Port establishments, was a night spot primarily. But she whispered.

"You know I do," he said.

"Can you get somebody to relieve you here?"

"For a few minutes?"

"For until I say different."

"I'll make a call." He did. "The relief guy will be here in twenty minutes. Can it wait till then?"

"Yes," she said, and took a table near the bar.

The new girl, Doris, a blonde of about twenty-five with dark roots and a nice frame and a pleasant, pockmarked face, waited on Julie; Julie ordered coffee. While Doris was off getting it, Julie came to the bar.

"Who is she?"

"Just some transient gal."

"Transient?"

"Divorcee. No kids. Got an ex-husband in Ohio she's on the run from."

"Why?"

"Cause he still loves her. Ever hear of that?"

"What did he do, beat her?"

"I guess."

Julie nodded and went back to the table. Doris brought the coffee.

Julie said, "You're new here, huh?"

Doris smiled, said, "Just collecting a few paychecks, honey. I'm on my way to California."

"Oh. Relatives there?"

"No. My folks are gone and I was the only one. I got a couple of old boyfriends out there, though. That's better than relatives."

"Any time. How's your paycheck collection coming along?"

"What do you mean?"

"I'm on my way to Los Angeles. Just stopped here to look up my ex-husband. He's that good-looking bartender over there."

"Harold's your ex? No kiddin'!"

She sat down.

"Say, I was mostly saving for my bus fare and such. If you can use a rider, somebody who can help you drive, I'll turn in my apron and hop in your car."

Julie smiled and extended a hand. "It's a deal."

Shortly before three o'clock that morning, Harold was in the Mustang, and Doris was behind the wheel. Harold, in the passenger's seat, was steering, because Doris was unconscious. Julie had put Seconal in some coffee Doris drank a few hours before. Harold was off on the shoulder, waiting for Julie. There was some snow on the ground, but no ice on the highway. It was cold. Harold was sweating.

She came over the bridge, driving his old sky-blue Dodge Charger, the one he'd had since college, and she blinked her brights. That meant the truck was coming. He pulled the Mustang across the mouth of the narrow bridge, left it in park, got out and ran to hop in Julie's waiting car. They were half a mile away when the small bridge behind them seemed to blow up, in a huge orange ball, as though a shell had hit it.

HE FINISHED the Manhattan and went out to her. It was chilly in the parking lot; there were no lights on out here, but the full moon provided some unreal-seeming illumination. She was standing with Ron, standing close. He pulled her away from Ron, who stood and watched them, that permanent, pouty snarl on her face.

He told Julie about the call from Infante.

They were talking about it when Ron noticed that kid, Jon, making a break for it, crawling away from her car toward the woods. The lez ran after the kid, dragged him back to the car, tossed him in.

Then Ron came back and said to Julie, "You oughta let me . . ."

"No," Julie said. "Take him to your place and sit on him."

Ron shrugged. "Okay," she said, and sauntered off to her '57 Ford and rumbled off.

"You're not going to kill that boy, are you?" Harold asked Julie.

"No."

"You mean Ron'll do it for you."

"I need him alive at the moment. Till we find out what Logan's up to."

"He'll come here. He's probably on his way right now."

"I can handle him."

"I don't think so. He sounds like one man you can't handle."

"We'll put this Infante to use."

"He doesn't sound like much. Some poor sappy kid. I'm afraid his partner was the smart one."

"He's the dead one now."

"True. Very true."

"Well, Harold. There's always you."

"I won't kill for you, Julie."

"Right," she said. She put her arm in his. "Let's lock up and go home. We can talk about it."

11

COOL CLOTH touched his face. It was soothing. Jon opened his eyes.

And looked into Ron's face.

For a moment the face looked almost human: the pouty mouth, the close-set eyes, were in a sort of repose, the nastiness set aside. Then she saw that he was awake and, with just a subtle shift, the features turned ugly again.

She stopped dabbing his face with the damp washrag; she pulled back.

"Don't stop," Jon said. "Feels good."

"You got bunged up," she said. Her tone was strangely apologetic. And almost a whisper. "I was cleaning off the dirt."

His face did hurt; even without touching it, he could feel the raw patches.

"Go ahead," he said. "That felt good, what you were doing."

She shrugged, with her shoulders and mouth both, and started touching his face again. Her touch was gentle. Which struck Jon as weird.

"I . . . I don't remember passing out," he said.

"You hit your head," she said.

"When?"

"When I tossed you in back of my car, after you tried to crawl off. You hit your head on the door. You got a bump."

He tried to feel his head, and his hand jerked, like a dog on a leash. He glanced over and saw that the hand was cuffed to the headboard of an old brass bed. His left hand was free, however, and he touched the bump on his head; it was sore, but it wasn't a big bump. On the side of his head, though, where she'd hit him with the gun barrel earlier, there was a real goose egg.

"You don't got a concussion or nothing," she said.

He was beginning to get his bearings. He was on his back, on the bed; his right hand was cuffed, and his left leg was, too, by the ankle. She was sitting on the edge of the bed, tending him. The room was dim: the only light on was a shaded lamp on the nightstand. This appeared to be a room in an older home. There was yellow floral wallpaper, faded, and paint was coming off the ceiling in spots, from water damage. Opposite the foot of the bed was an old dresser with mirror; on top of the dresser was a row of trophies of some sort. There was a door to the right; a window over to the left. It was an average-size bedroom. Nothing remarkable about it.

Except maybe for the pictures. The mirror over the dresser was covered with them, pin-ups taped to it, but not of girls: Elvis Presley, James Dean, Eddie Cochran; fifties teen faves, mostly dead. Some of the pictures were faded pages clipped from old magazines, the Scotch tape yellowed and dried; others looked more recent. It was a mirror you couldn't look into. But the faces on it looked back at you, peeking over the row of trophies.

She yanked the cloth away from his raw face. "What are you lookin' at?"

"Just the pictures. On the mirror."

"What about 'em?"

"Nothing. They're fine. They're fine."

Her face lost some of its nastiness, and she said, "You name's Jon, huh?"

"Right. And you're Ron."

"Yeah. Sounds like a poem, don't it? Jon and Ron." She laughed.

He found a little smile for her somewhere and forced something out of him that he hoped sounded like a laugh. *God, this dyke is nuts,* he thought.

"I'm, you know . . . sorry about this," she said. Sullenly.

"Sorry?"

She dragged it out of herself. "I . . . got nothing against you, really."

"You don't?"

"I used to come listen to you. Your band. You guys were good."

"Thanks."

"You played too much sixties. I like fifties."

"Uh, well, there's lots of requests for sixties stuff these days. But I like fifties music myself."

She smiled; the sullenness was gone. "I know. I heard you do 'Whole Lotta Shakin'.' Anybody that can do Jerry Lee that good is okay by me."

"I'm . . . glad you liked it."

"Look, I know I probably made a . . . bad impression that time, few months ago, when I got on your case for being with Darlene. I know it's not your fault. Darlene, she's always hitting on people."

He tried to think of something to say to that, but couldn't. He was trying to stay low key and calm, trying not to scream at her. She seemed relatively calm herself at the moment, and he had a feeling that keeping her that way might be to his benefit.

"Are you hungry?" she asked suddenly.

"I . . . hadn't really thought about it."

"Well, are you?" Nastier.

"Sure. Sure. If it . . . wouldn't be too much trouble."

"Naw! Not at all. How 'bout a ham sandwich and a beer?"

"That'd be . . . great."

"No problem," she said, smiling, rising. She sauntered over toward the door and out.

What a fucking fruitcake! he thought, and began to take toll of his situation. He took a look at the headboard of the bed. He was cuffed to one of its brass posts; there didn't seem to be any way to slide the cuff off the thing. And he certainly couldn't pull his wrist through the cuff.

He was able to get into a sitting position, but he could stay that way only by supporting himself with his free hand. It allowed him to see that his ankle (his shoes were off; he could see them over on the floor, by the dresser) was cuffed to the brass end rail of the bed.

For having an arm and a leg free, he was pretty goddamn helpless.

If he didn't feel so weak, he could try to overpower her; maybe knock her out with a punch when she got close, or kick her in the head or something. But then what?

Then she was there with the sandwich and beer, a Coors.

She'd taken off the leather jacket; she was in T-shirt and jeans now, her smallish breasts poking at her T-shirt in a reminder that she was female.

She handed him the sandwich and a paper napkin and said, "I put hot mustard on it."

"I like hot mustard."

"You got beer to wash it down with." She put the beer on the nightstand, since he didn't have a hand handy to take it.

He ate the sandwich. He was starving. He didn't realize it till he got the food in front of him, but he was starving.

She was smiling as she watched him eat. And not at all in a sinister way. The dimness of the room, with its single source of light, threw shadows on her and everything else, but the effect was softening.

When he was finished, she said, "Use another beer to wash that down better?"

"Uh. Sure. That'd be great."

This time she left the door open as she went, and he could see her going out into the hall and taking a right down some stairs; he could hear her feet on the stairs, and then again, a couple minutes later, coming back up.

She gave him a second Coors; she'd brought a beer for herself, too, but in a glass. She had an empty coffee can under her arm and set it on the floor by the bed.

"What's that for?" he asked.

"You can't buy beer, you can only rent it," she said.

"Oh."

"Can you reach it there?"

"I don't think so."

"With your hand, stupid."

He reached over with his left hand and could feel the lip of the can.

"Yeah," he said. "Thanks."

She sat on the edge of the bed again.

"How old are you?" she asked him.

"Twenty-one," he said.

"How old you think I am?"

Thirty.

"Twenty," he said.

"Twenty-five," she grinned, with a slight foam mustache.

Thirty.

"Fooled me," Jon said.

"I live right," she explained.

"Uh, Ron?"

"Yeah?"

"Why am I here?"

"How the fuck should I know?"

"Well. You did bring me here."

"Yeah. So?"

"Well, why'd you do it? Why am I tied up like this?"

"That's between you and Julie."

"Julie."

"Yeah. I'm only doing this 'cause she asked me to. I don't get no pleasure out of it."

"You don't."

"Fuck, no. You're a nice kid. You sing good. I like you."

"You do."

She smiled again—a real smile, with some gums showing, and disarming, in a weird fucking way. "Yeah. I don't always like guys, you know."

"You don't?"

"Nope. But I don't always like girls, either." She touched his leg.

He couldn't think of anything to say.

"You thought I was queer, didn't you?" she said.

"Oh. I don't know."

"I like girls. I like guys, too, sometimes. I don't know. Sometimes, it's . . . well, it's easier for me with girls."

"Is it easy with Julie?"

He'd crossed some line he shouldn't have. She pulled her hand away from his leg, and the nasty look returned. "Don't get cute, prick," she said.

"I didn't mean anything by it."

"You just better stay on my good side."

"Hey, I'm not here because I asked to be, you know."

"Yeah. I know. You got a better temper about it than I would, I guess."

"Do you work for Julie?"

"I do stuff for her. I'm kind of a night watchman at the Paddlewheel. Most of Gulf Port is all-night places, but Julie closes up at two. So I keep an eye on the place most nights."

"Not tonight."

"No. Tonight I'm keeping an eye on you."

"I see."

"If Julie wants me to sit on you, she's got her reasons. It's between the two of you. I got nothin' to do with it."

"How much do you know about her?"

Ron smiled. "I know her pretty well."

"She tried to kill me once. With a shotgun."

"Sure," she said, sipping her glass of Coors.

"We were in on a bank job together, and she tried to kill my partner and me."

"You? A bank robber? Don't make me choke."

"She took the money. Where do you think she got the money for the Paddlewheel, you dumb cunt? Then I saw her at the Barn, tonight, and she figures I'll tell my partner about her, and she's afraid he'll come after her."

That stopped Ron. For some reason—Jon's near-hysteria, perhaps—it had rung true to her.

"What'll he do, this guy?" she asked.

"I don't know. Now that she's kidnapped me, I don't know what he's liable to do."

"Kidnapped. Who's kidnapped?"

"I'm handcuffed to the goddamn bed, lady. What the fuck do you *think* this is?"

Ron got up, walked around.

"Julie said sit on you," she said. "I'm doing what she asked me to and that's all."

"I heard you. And I heard you say back at that parking lot you'd as soon kill me as look at me."

Ron turned and looked at him, and there was an expression on her face that could only be described as a mixture of pain and embarrassment. She came over and sat on the edge of the bed and picked up the washrag from the nightstand and touched a couple places on his face again. Then she put the washrag down and said, "That was just bullshit."

"Was it."

"I'm sorry about your face getting bunged up, and your head. I hit you with the gun pretty hard. I . . ."

She lowered her head.

"I show off sometimes," she said. "When somebody like Darlene's around . . . or somebody like Julie, especially Julie . . . I show off. I get tough. Act tough. Talk tough. Overdo it. Don't ask me why."

Why is she telling me this? Jon wondered.

"She's going to ask you to kill me," Jon said.

"Naw. It'll never happen."

"You've done things for her before."

"I roughed some people up for her before. Big deal."

"You kidnapped me tonight for her."

"Kidnapped! Nobody's been kidnapped."

"Ron. Let me go, before you get in this any deeper."

"Yeah, and you'd go to the cops."

"I can't go to the cops."

"Why, 'cause you're a bank robber? You're funny."

"Ron, Julie's going to call your bluff. She's going to ask you to kill me. Are you up to that?"

Ron thought about that.

"I'm tired of talkin'," she said, rising. "You get some sleep."

She switched off the lamp and left the room.

For about an hour, Jon worked at the cuffs, tried to see if the headboard of the bed could be unscrewed or otherwise come loose from the bed itself.

Then sun was coming in the window, and Ron was coming in the door. She was still wearing jeans and T-shirt and had a plate of eggs and ham in one hand and orange juice in the other.

"Did you sleep?" she asked.

"I guess," Jon said, not sure.

"If I give you this stuff, will you be good?"

"I won't try anything," he said.

"All right," she said, and gave him the food. She stood over by the dresser and leaned against it while he ate. She fingered one of the trophies on the dresser.

"This was my brother's room," she said. Out of nowhere.

"Really? Where is he now?"

"Dead."

"Uh. I'm sorry."

"Stock car accident. That's what the trophies are."

"I'm very sorry."

"He was about your age when he cracked up."

"Really? When was this?"

"Fifteen years ago, June."

"You must've loved him."

"Yeah. I thought a lot of him. He was what kept this place going."

"Oh?"

"I had three little sisters. My mom and dad drank, and Billy . . . my brother . . . he was tough. If Dad tried to hit one of us, he'd belt him. From about thirteen on he could beat the crap outa my old man."

"No kidding."

"When Billy got killed, I . . . kind of took over. Stepped in.

Otherwise my old man would've started in on us again. Boy, did it shock the shit out of *him*."

"What did?"

She laughed. "When he found out his little girl could beat the crap out of him too. He only stuck around about a year after that."

"Where's the rest of the family now?"

"Mom's dead. Bad liver. The girls are all married. One of 'em just this last summer. Too young: sixteen. I didn't raise her right, maybe. Pregnant. Oh well. Maybe she'll be happy."

In the distance, bells were sounding.

"It's Sunday," she said. "I'm gonna be gone a while. Think you can get along without me?"

"Do I have a choice? Where are you going?"

"Mass, stupid," she said.

She went out, shutting the door this time.

"Light a candle for me," Jon said.

James Dean and company stared at him while he struggled with the cuffs and the headboard. About fifteen minutes later, he heard her go out; he wondered what she looked like dressed for church. Then he got back to his struggling. And got nowhere. He fell asleep after a while.

He woke and it was dark in the room. It wasn't night: the shades were drawn. A little light crawled in under the shade and from around the edges, but the nightstand lamp was off, and there was no other light in the room.

She was standing near the bed. She wasn't wearing anything. Her body wasn't great, but it wasn't bad; she had a square-ish frame with modest breasts, but there was no fat on her. It was a supple, vaguely muscular body. She had a tattoo of a black rose near her right hipbone, just above her pubic thatch. Her pouty face didn't look pretty, exactly, but she wasn't ugly.

He didn't say anything as she undid his pants.

"No man ever made me come," she said. "Do you think you can, Jon?"

"I'll try," Jon managed.

She sat on him.

4

12

NOLAN ALMOST missed the sign.

It was over to the left, a barn-wood sign about four by four, with the following words painted on in faded red: "THE BARN, Turn Right." This was lit from beneath by two small floods.

He turned right, off the highway onto gravel. The road was narrow, its ditches deep, and to stay out of them, Nolan slowed to about thirty. He could see the structure up ahead, beyond the flattened cornfields, up to the right. It was stark in the moonlight, a barn with a tin shed growing out of it, like an outstretched arm.

In front of the barn was a graveled parking lot, and he pulled into it. There were no other cars in the lot. He got out of the little red Datsun, which he'd gotten from Sherry, tucking the silenced 9 mm, which he'd gotten from dead Sal, into his waistband. He hadn't taken time to change clothes—he was still wearing the corduroy jacket and turtleneck and slacks he'd worn to Iowa City today, though that seemed like a year ago—and he felt less than refreshed.

The drive from the Quad Cities had drained him. He'd had a long day, too much of it spent behind the wheel of a car, and the rest poring over the books with Wagner and the Pier's accountant, and drinking a little too much afterward. And then the shit had hit the fan, and he'd pulled the energy out of somewhere; the adrenalin had pumped and he'd managed to save that nice ass of Sherry's and rid the world of that cocksucker Sal, whose body he'd dumped on a side road between the Quad Cities and Port City.

Right now he felt every one of his fifty-odd years, after a cramped hour-and-a-half in a small car, on a rolling, narrow two-lane highway, watching for speed traps, popping No-Doz to force his alertness to an artificial edge.

He stood and stretched and looked at the barn that was the Barn, letting the chill air have at him. Between the full moon and a number of tall posts with outdoor lights, the exterior of the structure was well lit, though its windows were dark. He didn't bother trying the front, restaurant, entrance, but walked around to the side door.

He could see the rustic bar, with its booths and wanted posters, through the steel-cross-hatched window of die door; there were enough beer signs lit to get a look. Not a soul. He walked around the long tin shed—it seemed a block long—and found some more empty parking lot at the rear.

On the other side of the building, though, in still more parking lot, were several vehicles.

There was a big four-wheel drive, a Land Rover, two-tone tan; a snow plow; and a van.

The van was light blue with a painted logo on it that said "THE NODES."

Jon's group.

Jon's van.

Nolan slipped out of his shoes.

It hurt to walk on the gravel in his goddamn socks, but it was quiet. The van had no side windows, but there were windows in back. On his toes (ouch—fuck!) he could peek in. He saw a lumpy bundle on the floor, a blanket over some stuff, he guessed. *Could* be a small person sleeping. He couldn't tell.

He looked in the front windows; the driver's and rider's seats were empty. He quietly tried the doors on either side. Locked.

Now what?

Somebody was in the Barn. There had to be, or the owners were goddamn dumb. A big place like this, stuck between a couple of cornfields, full of booze and other inventory, not to mention furniture and fixtures—hell, there *had* to be a sleep-in watchman. Without one, you'd go broke in a week.

So somebody was in there—somebody who belonged to the tan Land Rover.

Which meant Nolan could go to a door and start banging his fist till somebody inside answered. And that somebody *might* know something about the abandoned Nodes van. Julie couldn't have grabbed the whole goddamn *band*, could she?

He went to the nearest door, which wasn't far from the parked Land Rover, and stopped.

Jon's phone call had brought him here, but Jon was, obviously, in trouble. The kind of trouble Sherry had been in, no doubt, or worse. What guarantee was there that Nolan wasn't walking into some setup right now? Knocking, announcing himself, could be very stupid. . . .

He went to the Land Rover and lifted the hood.

It took about thirty seconds for the sound of the sticking, blaring horn to get a reaction inside the building. A dog barked; some lights went on; movement within. Nolan was waiting, his back to the building, to the right of the door, 9 mm in hand, as the man looked out—a big man, tall, wearing a hunting jacket over a bare chest and shiny blue pajama bottoms. He had a shotgun.

The man was only partway out, the door open, leaning

toward the Land Rover and its blaring horn; he didn't see Nolan, who was behind the partly open door. That was good.

Not good was the snarling dog on the other side of that door, a big dog, from the sound of it, who may not have seen Nolan but obviously sensed him, and knew *exactly* where he was.

Fortunately, the dog was unable to transfer its knowledge to his owner, who said, "Stay back, Queenie—I'll let you know if I need you."

But Queenie had a mind of her own, and as the man stepped out of the doorway onto the gravel, Queenie lurched forward.

Just as she did, Nolan shut the door on the bitch, hard, catching the snapping animal by the shoulders, lodging it there.

"Order it back!" Nolan said, shoulder pushing against the door. The dog, which had shut up for a second, caught by surprise and pain, was barking hysterically, trying to get its big German Shepherd head around to where she could bite off Nolan's left hand, on the door knob. Above it all, the Land Rover's horn was going as though this was a jail break.

The guy was standing there, his back to Nolan, but partially turned, glancing over his shoulder to see the gun in Nolan's right hand. His own shotgun was slack in his hands.

"Order it back, I said," Nolan said, straining against the door.

"Queenie," the man said. "Get back."

The dog's snapping turned into a quiet growl.

"Get back, Queenie."

The dog pulled back.

Nolan shut the door. Behind it the dog still growled. Even the blare of the Land Rover's horn couldn't drown it out.

The big man in hunting jacket and pajama bottoms twitched, as if about to turn.

Nolan said, "You can't turn fast enough."

The guy kept his back to Nolan but turned his head just enough to give Nolan a "Fuck you" look.

Nolan said, "Toss the shotgun. Toss it good."

The guy tossed it.

"Go fix your horn," Nolan said.

The guy walked slowly toward the Land Rover. Nolan followed. The guy lifted the hood, stopped the blaring. He shut the hood, then turned and looked at Nolan and said, "I'm gonna . . ."

"You're going to shut up," Nolan said.

The guy did.

"I'm not a thief," Nolan said, which wasn't exactly true, but in this case was. "I'm not here to cause you any harm."

"Go to hell."

"Lean back against the four-wheel. Put your hands on the hood."

He did.

"What's your name?" Nolan asked.

"Fuck you."

"Don't be stupid. This isn't a contest."

"Bob Hale."

"You the watchman?"

He bristled. "I *own* the damn place."

"No offense. This van here."

"What about it?"

"It's the band's, isn't it? The band that played here tonight, correct?"

"Yeah. Correct."

"What's it doing here?"

"I don't know. I'm surprised it's still here myself."

Nolan was afraid of that.

"Some of 'em loaded some equipment in a trailer and left," Hale was saying. "They said the other guy would probably be by tomorrow for his amplifiers and shit, which is still inside."

"The other guy."

"Jon. The leader. Had a chance to get laid or something and bugged out. He'll turn up for his stuff tomorrow."

There was a sound behind Nolan; he turned, quick, and saw the rear doors of the Nodes van open up.

"Get out slow," Nolan said. He was standing with his back to the building, which he didn't like doing, but it allowed him to keep an eye on both Hale, by the Land Rover, and whoever it was climbing out of the Nodes van.

"Let's see your hands," Nolan ordered. "Over your head."

It was a girl. A young woman in a denim jacket and jeans. So the bundle under the blanket *had* been a small, sleeping person.

"I wanted to make sure it was you," she said. She was staying near the van. A busty little brunette with a pretty, heart-shaped face.

"You're Jon's girl, aren't you?" Nolan said.

"Not his girl, exactly," she said, shrugging. "But I'm who you think I am. I think."

"Toni, isn't it?"

"Yes," she said. She seemed surprised that he remembered her name. And a little pleased. "Can I put my hands down?"

"Yes, and come over here."

She went to Hale.

"Bob," she said, putting a hand on his arm, which was still leaning back so he could keep his hands on the Land Rover's hood, per Nolan's instructions, "this is a friend of Jon's. I didn't want to worry you before, Bob . . . but something's happened to Jon."

He looked confused. "What are you talking about?"

"Somebody's kidnapped him, I think," Toni said.

"Did you call the cops?" Hale asked.

"Can't," Toni said.

"Better be quiet," Nolan told her.

"Why can't you?" Hale asked.

Nolan raised his gun.

"Just asking," Hale said.

Nolan looked at Toni. She nodded. He looked at Hale. He said, "Jon and I are involved with some people who wouldn't like the police involved. You don't want to know any more than that."

"You're right," Hale said.

"I'll put my gun away if you'll take us inside and keep your dog off."

"Okay." Hale shrugged.

"Go get his shotgun," Nolan told Toni.

She did.

Nolan broke it open, handed the shells to Hale, then handed him the empty gun as well.

He turned to Toni. "Get my shoes, would you?"

"You're in your stocking feet!"

"That's why I want my shoes." He pointed to them.

She got them for him. He put them on.

Then Hale led them into the Barn, commanding his surly dog to heel, which it did, reluctantly.

Hale took them out into the bar, where he turned on some lights. The dog headed for a nearby pinball machine and curled up beneath it and slept; even in repose, it looked like a killer. Nolan asked Hale if he had some coffee. Hale asked if instant was okay and Nolan said fine.

While Hale got the coffee, Nolan got the story of what had happened here, from Toni's point of view.

"When Jon never got back," she said, "I went out and found the van was still here. I couldn't think of anything to do but hope you got Jon's message, and wait for you to show up."

"So you waited in the van."

"Yeah, but I fell asleep and didn't hear you get here. Didn't hear you prowling around, either. You say you tried the doors on the van?"

"The ones up front, yes."

"And I slept right through it. I'm not very good at this, am I?"

"Well, you're new at it. And I'm quiet."

"Yeah, you sneak around in your socks. I didn't wake up till that horn started in. Scared the shit out of me, too."

"So Julie runs a gambling joint," Nolan said. "That explains the Chicago connection."

"What?"

Nolan shushed her, as Hale joined them in the booth with the coffee. The big man seemed almost friendly now. He had even taken the time to put some money in the jukebox; Charlie

Daniels was singing something mournful at the moment. But it did serve to give a social flavor to this forced meeting.

And Hale clearly liked Toni; he looked at her with an obvious, though somehow childish, lust.

"Why'd you stay out in that van?" Hale asked her. "If I'd known you was in trouble, you could've come stayed in my pad."

"I never thought of that," she said with a straight face.

"Toni says this woman—this Julie," Nolan said, as if he didn't know who Julie was, "asked about Jon."

"Yeah. She was interested in booking 'em over at her club."

"His band, you mean."

"Yeah. She has quite the place, over there by Gulf Port."

"Tell me about it—the Paddlewheel."

"I suppose I could. I could also call Julie, after you leave, and tell her you was asking about her, you know."

Toni touched Hale's arm again. "Please don't."

"You don't want in this any deeper than you already are," Nolan told him. It wasn't exactly a threat.

Hale thought about that.

Then he said, "Okay, you convinced me. Ask me what you want and get out of here. I want to get back to bed. Listening to that dog is making me sleepy."

Over under the pinball machine, his dog was snoring.

"You know," Hale said, "you could just as easy killed that bitch of mine out there. But you didn't. Maybe that says something about you."

"Maybe it does," Nolan said.

13

THE DOUBLE bed, covered by a garish green and red floral spread, came out of the wall at right; a TV and dresser with mirror were against the wall at left. There was just enough room between for Infante to pace.

It was a dingy little room, with smudged-looking yellow plaster walls and a green shag carpet speckled with dirt; over the bed was a picture of two horses running. Tacky, Infante thought. Just the sort of depressing room he didn't need right now. But he had no choice but to be here; this was where that guy Harold said to come. Besides which, there wasn't any other motel in Gulf Port.

Infante had rolled in just after three and had driven around a little bit, checking it out, and found Gulf Port wasn't a town at all, not really—just a collection of trailers and shacks, no business section or anything. If there hadn't been a full moon, he wouldn't have been able to see the town, hardly, which would have been okay with him.

Scattered along the outskirts of Gulf Port, though, were eight or ten bars, all thriving, and that explained it: Gulf Port wasn't a town, it was a watering hole, a place to go when the bars across the river closed up at two.

The motel was down the road from a place called Upper's, a big one-story brown brick country rock joint with a hundred cars in the lot. The neon sign in front of the motel said "EEZER INN" in pulsing orange. Cute, Infante thought. The woman at the check-in desk was chubby and about fifty-five, with a lot of makeup and perfume and a frilly white blouse unbuttoned enough to show the start of big, withering boobs. Sickening. Ex-whore, he supposed. She was reading a Harlequin paperback. She'd tried giving him a sexy smile as she handed his room key over to him, and it all but made him barf.

There were ten units in front and another ten in back, and about half of them were full up. He'd asked for one in back, and now he was pacing around inside the dreary little cubicle, feeling as unappealing as the desk clerk and as dirty as the room itself.

He hadn't had time to grab any of his things before leaving. He was still in the black outfit he had worn with Sally when they went in after Nolan's bitch. He felt dirty. He needed a shave. He considered taking a shower, but then he'd just have to get back in these sweaty clothes, and he couldn't stand the thought of that.

He'd shower after his employers, the man Harold and the

woman Julie, had come and gone. He had called them as soon as he got in the room, which was five minutes ago; they should be here any time now.

He stopped pacing. He sat on the double bed, with his back to the running horses. The silenced 9 mm in his waistband nudged him, and he took it out and put it beside him, on the bed. Then he sat leaning forward, his elbows on his knees, forehead against the palms of his hands. He felt very alone. He missed Sally.

"I'm going to kill that fucker," he said. To himself. Through his teeth.

He sat up. He could see himself in the dresser mirror. He looked bad—scroungy. But he looked at himself, pointed a finger at himself, and said, "Understand? *Kill* the fucker!"

There was a knock at the door.

He got up, took the gun with him just in case, cracked the door (there was no night latch), and it was a sandy-haired man in dark-rimmed glasses, big—not tall, but big—and good-looking, in a rough way. He was wearing a yellow sports shirt and tan slacks. Smelled of Brut.

"You're Infante," the man said.

"You're Harold."

"Right." The big man turned and motioned to somebody in the car pulled in next to Infante's jet-black Mazda. The car was a cream-color Porsche. Which said class. Which also said money. Maybe this wasn't such a bad crowd to be in with after all, Infante thought.

A woman got out. She was wearing black slacks and a silky blouse, tits flopping. Handsome enough woman, he supposed. Nice clothes, anyway.

The. guy went to her; he had a fluid walk, like an athlete. Put an arm around her. He was a muscular sort—big shoulders. Works with weights. Infante bet.

The two of them came in.

Infante closed and locked the door and stuck the gun back in his waistband and said, "This place is a dump, in case you missed it."

The woman, Julie, turned to him and smiled. It was an attractive smile, not that he gave a damn. "I'm sorry we couldn't do better for you," she said. "Gulf Port isn't exactly Las Vegas, you know."

"That's not the way I heard it," Infante said.

"If you mean the Paddlewheel, it's not in Gulf Port proper. It's a few miles from here, on the river."

"You wouldn't think people running a classy place like that would stick a friend in a dump like this."

The man, Harold, sat on the bed. "Infante, this is only temporary. . . ."

"Put me up in the Holiday Inn across the river, then, back in Burlington. I'm allergic to cockroaches."

Julie touched his arm, and he batted it away.

"Excuse me," she said, searching his face. "You see, we need to have you close at hand. We need you here."

"Yeah, well, we'll see."

"I think we have mutual interests. Sit down, won't you?" She gestured toward the space on the double bed, next to Harold. Infante sat down.

"Harold said your partner was killed," the woman said.

"Yeah. Yeah he was killed. Goddammit."

"This man Logan . . ."

"His name is Nolan."

"Nolan, then. He did it."

"Yeah he did it."

"And you want even."

"Of course I want even. What kind of guy do you think I am?"

She seemed to think about that for a moment, then said, "We're going to pay you what we promised, even though you and your partner didn't exactly . . . succeed."

Infante sighed. "Look. I gotta admit something. Sally handled the business end. I don't even know what you promised us. Sally was the brains, I have to say."

The woman walked back and forth, slowly, thinking, smiling. "Then why don't we just start over? Why don't we pick a new figure? How's ten thousand dollars?"

"Ten . . ."

"That's a lot of money, isn't it?"

"It sure . . ."

"Enough for you to disappear for a while?"

"Sure."

"Then you'll do it?"

"Do what?"

"Kill Nolan."

"Try and stop me!"

"Oh," she smiled, not pacing, stopping in front of him, "I'm not about to do that."

Next to him, the big guy seemed glum. Sensitive face, Infante thought.

"Now," she was saying, "when can we expect him to arrive?"

"Nolan? I'd say . . . couple days. Late tomorrow at the soonest."

Harold said, "How do you figure that?"

"He's got Family friends. He'll want to check with 'em about who sent us. They'll be able to find out too, pretty easy."

"Couldn't he do that with just a phone call?" Julie asked. "Couldn't he be on his way here right now?"

"I don't see how," Infante said. "All he knows is two Family boys tried to kill him. He's going to figure, at first, that he's on the shit list for some reason. Which'll send him off in the wrong direction. He'll go to Chicago and hit on a few people in person till he finds out what's going on."

Julie was nodding. "You're right" she said. "I know this man; that's what he'd do."

Harold said to Infante, "How long will it take him?"

Infante shrugged. "Once he knows the Family didn't send us, he'll find you. No question. He's in tight with some pretty high-up people. A few phone calls, and they'll have you cold."

"Julie," Harold said, "*you've* got Chicago connections. That's how we got hold of Infante and his partner. Couldn't you . . ."

"Sorry," Infante interrupted, "but any connections you got are much smaller shots than the people Nolan's tight with. The guy I work for, Mr. Hines, who is in the Bahamas at the moment, didn't like it when this Nolan came to the Quad Cities, opening up a club. He complained and pretty soon there was a phone call. From a guy named Felix. He's nobody you ever heard of, but what Sally told me is he's like the corporate lawyer for the Family. And he told Mr. Hines that Nolan was a personal friend. So Nolan's well connected, all right."

"Shit," Julie said. She wasn't smiling now.

Harold said to her, "That means you can't turn to your Chicago friends for help."

"I don't dare to, no, dammit," she said. She had a hand on one hip and rubbed her forehead with her other hand.

"If Nolan's connected," Harold continued, "killing . . . killing him might cause you trouble. Family trouble."

She shot the man a look that said he was saying too much in front of a relative outsider like Infante.

But Harold pressed on. "You could leave," he suggested.

"Don't be silly."

"He's right," Infante said. "Just take off. Your boyfriend and me can handle Nolan." Infante patted Harold's shoulder. "We'll let you know when the smoke clears."

She laughed. "I told you I *know* this man, Logan, Nolan, whatever. He's not easily handled. But he does have a weakness."

"What's that?" Infante said.

"Harold," Julie said, "I'm kind of parched. Get us some Cokes from the machine, would you?"

Harold shrugged, rose; Infante watched the man walk to the door. Graceful for a big guy. He went out.

She sat on the bed next to Infante. She didn't touch him, but kept her distance.

"Harold's a bit squeamish," she said.

"A lot of big guys are soft at the center," Infante said.

"Harold has his strong points."

"I bet he does."

"I just don't want him hearing what I'm going to tell you."

"Okay."

"Nolan's got this friend. This close friend."

"Yeah, so?"

"It's this kid, about twenty. Muscular, curly haired little guy. Cute."

"Yeah?"

"And they're close friends. You catch my drift yet?"

"You mean . . . Nolan and this kid? . . ."

"Right."

"He's living with a broad, for Christ's sake."

"So what?"

Infante thought about that, said, "Yeah, right. So he's double-gaited, so what about it?"

"So I got the kid."

Infante grinned. "No shit?"

"None at all. I'm keeping him at a place just a few miles from here."

"He's your guest, only it wasn't his idea, you mean."

"Right. A friend of mine's sitting on him."

"I'm liking the sound of this. Go on."

"I'm not leaving. Or hiding, or anything. I'm waiting for Nolan to show up, and then I'm going to use the kid on him."

"How?"

"I'll make Nolan an offer. He figures I owe him, from a past thing. And he won't be thrilled I sent you and your partner after him. But he likes money. He can be bought. And he likes this kid."

"So, you'll settle up with him?"

"I'll offer him money and give the kid back; all he has to do is just go away."

"Will he buy that?"

"He'll do what he has to to get the kid. And the money won't hurt."

"I take it he doesn't know yet that you have this kid?"

Julie smiled. "We grabbed him before he had a chance to get a message out."

"Where do I come in?"

"When I hand the kid over to him, you'll kill them both. Any problem with that?"

"No. How's it going to work, exactly?"

The door opened.

Harold was back with the Cokes. He passed the cans around, and everybody sipped at them. Julie took two slow drinks of hers, then put it on the dresser.

"I'll be back in touch," she said.

Harold looked a little confused.

She headed for the door, and Harold, looking back at Infante suspiciously, followed.

"Get some sleep," she told Infante, and they were gone.

He sat on the bed. The gun nudged his belly again, and he took it out of his waistband and laid it on the bed, next to him, gently. Ten thousand dollars. He smiled.

He took his shower. Hot, steaming shower. He was starting to feel better. Every few minutes, though, he had a grief pang; he came out of the bathroom, towel wrapped around him, and saw the empty double bed and couldn't hold back the tears.

He sat on the edge of the bed and cried, his body trembling. Now and then rage would flood through him and he'd say, "*Kill the fucker.*"

He was doing this when another knock came at the door.

He rubbed his hand across his face.

So the woman was back. She ditched the hunk and was going to fill him in on the details. Fine.

He took the gun with him, just in case it wasn't Julie, and went to the door and cracked it open, and it wasn't Julie.

It was Nolan.

14

IT WAS well after four in the morning when Nolan let Bob Hale and his dog go back to sleep, and headed out for Sherry's Datsun in the Barn parking lot. The girl, Toni, followed him. He opened the door on the driver's side, and the girl grabbed his forearm.

"I'm going with you," she said.

He didn't say anything.

"I'm not going to argue with you. I'm going. And that's the end of it."

He didn't say anything.

"You need me. I been to Gulf Port before—know my way around the bars. I know how to find Darlene. That's the little cunt that tricked Jon into going out to the van for a quickie. She had to be in on it, or at least see what happened, see who grabbed him."

He didn't say anything.

"I can find her. I know she hangs around the bars in Gulf Port. Seems to me she might even live there; if not, across the river in Burlington. I can find her. And if you find her, you find Jon. So I'm going. You need me, and I'm not going to argue with you."

"Get in," Nolan said.

"What?"

"Get in. We're wasting time standing here yakking."

"I'm going?"

"Of course you're going. I wouldn't have it any other way." He smiled at her, just a little. "Get in."

She got in.

It was only ten minutes to Burlington, a city on rolling hills overlooking the Mississippi, an industrial town of thirty-some thousand, whose various facelifts did not conceal its age. A freeway, lined with shelves of ivy-covered shale, cut through the old river town, and after paying the thirty cents round-trip toll, they were rumbling over the steel bridge, to Illinois and Gulf Port.

The sign just beyond the bridge directed them to the left, but the road curved around to the right, finally depositing them in a pocket below the busy interstate, where Gulf Port rested like a wound that hadn't healed properly.

On first impression, Gulf Port was nothing but bars. Bars with big parking lots full of cars and trucks. Even just driving by, it was clear just how rowdy these places were, drunks and loud music constantly tumbling out the doors. In the background, among trees that hid the river, he could make out the towers of a grain elevator, which seemed to be the only business of any consequence in Gulf Port that didn't serve beer. He drove through the narrow, unpaved streets and found that this was little more than a trailer court, with an occasional sagging house thrown in for variety. No grocery store; no business section at all. He hadn't even seen a gas station yet, though there probably was one among the bars.

"Shitty place to visit, and I wouldn't want to live here," the girl commented. It was the first thing she'd said since they left the Barn.

Nolan nodded. "Welfare ghetto, looks like."

He drove back toward the bars.

"According to Hale," he said, "these bars'll be open till five. That doesn't give you much time to spot this Darlene."

"It should be enough. There's a bar on the farthest end of town, about the nicest one. It's called Upper's. Turn here."

He did.

"It's down there. See the sign?"

He saw it: a standing metal sign that in blue neon said "UPPER'S" at the front of a large parking lot. He pulled in. The lot was eighty percent full. A few well- plastered customers, men in their twenties in jeans and western-style jackets, with the long hair that once would have branded them hippies but now probably meant young blue-collar worker, were pushing each other around and laughing, just outside the front door. The building itself was a low-slung brick building, brown, with a tile roof; a big place, despite being only one story. The front door was closed at the moment, but it didn't entirely muffle the country-rock music within.

"She'll be in there if she's anywhere," the girl said.

"If she isn't?"

"If she isn't, she's in the sack with some low-life. That's my guess, anyway."

"Hooker?"

"I think a few beers is all she costs. But it's possible she's hooking."

"How sure are you she lives here?"

"If she doesn't, she lives back in Burlington. She and that dyke I told you about were at the Burlington gigs the Nodes played."

"Okay. I want you to go in and see if she's in there."

"And?"

"And then we're going to wait and follow her home."

"Why don't I just corner her in the ladies' can or something?"

"Once we've talked to her, we'll have to shut her up."

The girl winced. "You don't mean . . ."

"No, I don't mean that. But we got to tie her up and gag her. Which if she's hooking is probably part of her scene anyway."

She smiled. "You're funny."

"A riot."

"We're going to get Jon, aren't we? He's going to be all right, right?"

"I don't know. I'm not promising you anything."

"He'll be all right. I know he will."

"Listen. Toni, isn't it? You got to face something: he may be dead right now."

She swallowed hard; her eyes looked wide and wet. Pretty little thing, Nolan thought.

"That's the kind of people we're dealing with," he said. "I'm sorry it's the case, but it is the case. Now. Go in there and see if that bitch is getting beers bought for her."

She nodded, got out. She had a nice rear end on her, Nolan noted clinically.

He sat and waited. He was tired. He rolled the window down, and the cold air felt good. He'd trade his left nut for an hour's sleep. But the stream of drunks and near-drunks coming in and out of the place, plus the country-rock music in the background, served to keep him from dropping off, and then the girl was back.

"She's in there," she said. Smiling like a conspirator.

"Fine."

"What now?"

"We wait."

"And follow her home."

"Right."

They sat there for ten minutes.

"Are you okay?" she said.

"I'm fine. Why?"

"You look like you're ready to fall asleep."

"That's because I'm fifty years old and been up a like number of hours."

"Well, I can watch for her. You sleep."

"Thanks, no thanks."

She patted his arm. "Jon's going to be all right."

He said nothing.

Five minutes later, a rather tall, heavily made-up girl with shaggy brunette hair, wearing a black down-filled jacket over a Marshall Tucker T-shirt and tight jeans, walked out arm in arm with a big, somewhat drunk guy in a cowboy hat, padded cowhide vest, and jeans.

"That's her," Toni said.

The couple swayed to a red truck, one of those hotrod pickups on the other side of the lot and the big guy stumbled behind the wheel as she got in on the rider's side and they pulled out. Nolan followed.

It wasn't far; in a "town" the size of Gulf Port, it couldn't be. The trailer was one of half a dozen others on a desolate, somewhat shaded block two blocks from Upper's. This apparently allowed Darlene to do her local bar-crawling without taking her car, because a several-year-old green Maverick was parked in front; rust was eating it. She guided the cowboy out of his pickup, up the couple of steps and inside.

"Well?" Toni said as they drove past.

"Let's wait till the pickup leaves," Nolan said.

"Shouldn't we . . . ?"

"We'll talk to her by herself. We don't need to involve any

civilians. This is complicated enough as is. We know where she lives. We'll come back later."

"That guy'll be there all night!"

"Right."

He pulled over. "I'm getting in back," he told her. "I'll keep down. I want you to drive to that motel down from Upper's and get a room. It's the only motel in town, and they may be watching for me for Julie. So you get the room."

She nodded, and they got out, and he got in back and she got behind the wheel.

Soon they were in the motel room, a dingy little yellow room with a double bed and a picture of a ship at sea over the bed. Toni appraised the latter and said, "At least it isn't on black velvet."

"What?" Nolan said.

"Nothing. What are we doing here?"

"I'm getting some sleep. You can do what you want."

"But what about Jon? Shouldn't we be . . ."

"If they've killed him, it won't matter. If he's alive, they'll probably keep him that way. But if I don't get a couple hours sleep, I'm liable to fuck up. Okay?"

"Don't pretend to be such a cold fucker, Nolan. You aren't fooling anybody."

"Then I'm not fooling anybody." He lay on the bed and closed his eyes.

"When should I wake you up?" she said.

"I'll wake up in a few hours. Why don't you sleep, too?"

"How can you sleep at a time like this?"

"It's hard with you talking."

"What about Darlene?"

"The cowboy'll be out of there by noon, probably. We'll call on her then."

"What if she gets up before then? What if she leaves?"

"Where would she go? Church?"

"She could go somewhere in the afternoon. Shopping in Burlington."

"She'll be back, then. Are the bars open here on Sunday?"

"Yeah."

"She'll be back."

"Yeah. I suppose you're right. Nolan."

"What?"

"Can I lay down on the bed?"

"There's only one bed."

"Does that mean yes?"

"It's a double bed, isn't it?"

"That means yes." She lay down.

A few minutes went by.

"You're not asleep yet, are you?" she asked him.

"Apparently not."

"Am I bothering you?"

"No." His eyes were closed.

"You're tense."

"I'm fine." He rolled over on his stomach.

He felt her hands on his shoulders, on the muscles between his neck and shoulders. She began rubbing. "You are too tense," she said. It felt good.

"Well, maybe I am," he said.

"Does that feel good?"

"Keep doing it," he said.

She rubbed. Then she untucked his shirt and reached her hands up under it and scratched.

"How's that feel?"

"Good."

"Just good?"

"Very good."

"I thought you were human."

"Why, is that news?"

"I just never knew a man who didn't like his back scratched."

She stopped and he turned over and leaned against his elbow and smiled at her. She was a cute kid; nice tits with the nipples poking at the Nodes T-shirt.

"Turn over," he said.

She grinned and got on her stomach. He rubbed her back a while; then he reached his hand under the T-shirt and scratched her back. She made contented sounds, like a purring kitten.

He slapped her butt and she yelped.

"Looks like you're human, too," he said.

She turned over and smiled up at him; took his hands and put them up under her shirt, in front this time.

"Hey," he said.

"What?" she said.

He didn't pull his hands away; he liked them where they were.

"You're Jon's girlfriend," he said.

"I'm not his girlfriend. I'm his friend."

"Just a fellow band member, huh?"

"That's right."

She kissed him. Slow, sweet kiss.

He looked at her, pushed her away from him, hands still under her shirt; she had a scared look.

"I need to be close to somebody right now," she said. "And I don't think it would hurt you, either."

She pulled her T-shirt off; her breasts looked just as nice as they felt.

He turned off the light. He took off his clothes, and she took hers off, too. They got under the covers and made love; it was slow and rather sweet. Like the kiss. She was right: it was exactly what he needed right now.

Afterwards, he sat up in bed and said, "Are you sure you're not Jon's girlfriend?"

"I care about him a great deal."

"You've never slept with him?"

"I didn't say that."

He shook his head, smiled disgustedly. "I been had."

"Me too," she said. "Listen, I'm thirsty."

"There's a pop machine a few doors down."

"I'd rather have Cutty Sark."

"I bet you would. Will you settle for a Coke?"

"Sure," she said. "You don't really mean you're going to go get it for me?"

He shrugged. "You scratch my back . . ."

He put his clothes on. As an afterthought, he stuck the silenced 9 mm in his waistband.

"Do you need that?" she asked, wide-eyed.

"No," Nolan said, meaning it. "I'm just being paranoid."

The night air—actually early morning air—was still cold, and he still liked the feel of it, the alertness it gave him. He hadn't managed to get any sleep yet, after all. But the girl had done him good. She had released some of his tension, though he found himself feeling guilty, as if he'd somehow betrayed Sherry. Which was crazy. He wasn't married. But he didn't suppose this Toni could understand how he felt, not with the strange sense of morality she and that generation of hers seemed to have.

As he was nearing the Coke machine, he noticed a car parked in the stall in front of one of the other rooms: a shiny black Mazda. Sporty little car, but it wasn't the car that caught his eye—it was the license plate. Even though this was Illinois, most of the plates on the cars in the motel stalls were Iowa ones; this one was Illinois, specifically Rock Island County.

Infante.

Nolan had left his LTD home, with its Rock Island plates, for just this reason; he'd suffered the discomfort of Sherry's little Datsun because its Ohio plates wouldn't lead anybody to him.

But Infante was dumb. Which became even more obvious when Nolan found the car unlocked. He checked the registration; the car belonged to Carl R. Hines, Infante's boss.

Nolan took the 9 mm out of his waistband.

He went to the door of the room the Mazda was parked in front of. He knocked.

Infante answered the door wearing a towel, which he held around him with one hand; in the other was the twin to Nolan's 9 mm, but he was too startled and slow for it to do him any good.

Before Infante knew what was happening, Nolan slapped him

across the face with the automatic, knocking him back into the room, the 9 mm's twin tumbling out of Infante's hands, leaving him sitting on the floor with the towel a puddle across his lap, rubbing his face and saying, "Shit! Shit!"

Nolan shut the door.

Infante said, "You fucker!"

"Shut up."

Infante started to get up.

Nolan pointed the 9 mm at Infante's head. "Keep your seat," he said.

Infante's eyes darted around, looking for his 9 mm.

"It's under the bed," Nolan said. "I don't think you can get to it in time."

"I'm going to kill you, you fucker."

"I don't think so."

"How did you get here so fast?"

"Weren't you expecting me?"

"Not for a couple days. I figured first you'd go to Chicago and check on why we tried to hit you."

"That's pretty smart—for you, Infante. But, no, I already know who sent you: a bitch named Julie, with a heart as big as all indoors."

"She'll kill you if I don't, Nolan. She's smart. Too smart for you."

"We'll see. Where's Jon?"

Infante grinned. "Your lover boy?"

"My what?"

"Julie told me about you two. I'm gonna kill him, too. I'm gonna feed him your dead dick, first. He'll like that."

Nolan laughed. "Julie is smart. She's been pushing the right buttons where you're concerned, obviously."

"What do you mean?"

"Never mind. What was the plan, Infante? Was she going to wait for me to show up, then try to trade Jon to me, in return for leaving her the hell alone?"

Infante looked disappointed. "Maybe," he said.

"And then she was going to have you hit us both."

Infante grinned again. "Maybe."

"Where's Jon?"

"Fuck you, fucker."

"Don't tell me. I don't want you to tell me. I'd rather tie you in a chair and burn the bottoms of your feet till you tell me."

That made Infante nervous. "I tell you, I don't know where he is. Somebody, some friend of hers, is keeping him. All I know is it's not far from here."

"Is that the truth? Believe me, I'd get a kick out of burning your fucking feet."

"It's the truth! I don't know where the fuck he is."

Nolan nodded; he believed Infante. Goddammit.

And Infante whipped the towel off his lap and at Nolan's face, and it stung, stunning him, and the naked Infante was on him, and Nolan went over backwards.

Then Nolan was on his back, and Infante's hands were on Nolan's throat squeezing, and the world was turning red.

"You shouldn't have killed Sally, you fucker! You shouldn't have killed Sally!"

Nolan fired the 9 mm, and Infante took it in the gut; his hands loosened around Nolan's neck, and Nolan pushed him off. Infante lay on the floor like a fetus, clutching his stomach, looking up at Nolan, dying.

"You shouldn't have killed Sally," Infante whimpered.

"You shouldn't have killed my dog," Nolan said.

15

BY midafternoon, Jon wasn't afraid of her anymore.

She was really just this poor, sad person, Ron was, somebody who got stuck with the responsibility of her family in such a way that it, well, made a man out of her. She wasn't stupid, though smart wasn't the word for her, either. Just this poor, uneducated, pathetic case, who he'd feel very sorry for if she didn't have him handcuffed to a bed in what was apparently an old house out in the country somewhere.

He guessed he'd been raped. It was a new experience for him, maybe even a learning experience: he understood better what women had been going through all these years. Still, he had a hunch he could put up with being raped better than most women would, as long as it wasn't a man doing it.

If he'd been pressed about it he'd have to admit that he'd found some enjoyment in it This strange, hungry, mannish woman sitting on him, grinding, coming like crazy, which was the good part: that made her beholden to him, in a way. Afterwards, still on top of him, she'd smiled and stroked his cheek and then suddenly her face had fallen and she seemed embarrassed or something, and got off him and ran out of the room, scooping up her clothes as she went.

She came back in T-shirt and jeans, with breakfast.

"It's afternoon," she said, shrugging, "but I figured maybe you oughta have something to eat, and . . . I don't know . . . this seemed right."

She'd made him sourdough pancakes and link sausages and American fries. On a nice plate, with a big glass of orange juice. It looked great. She had it on a tray, which she handed him.

"How about undoing this?" he said, nodding toward his cuffed hand.

She shook her head no. "Can't do that." She seemed embarrassed about that, too.

She went over and let up the shade, and sun came in.

He ate the breakfast.

"This is terrific," he said.

She sat on the edge of the bed, watching him, smiling just barely; saying nothing.

When he was done, she took the tray away and was gone for over an hour. At one point he heard water running. Was she taking a bath? Then he heard a hair dryer.

When she returned, she was wearing a white peasant blouse,

lacy in front with long sleeves; and jeans. She had a little makeup on: pale lipstick; blush on her cheeks. Her head was a mess of curls: ducktail no more; she had hot-curled her hair, evidently, after washing it. The perfume she had on was a little strong, an evergreen fragrance, like a room deodorizer, and it hit him as soon as she stepped in the room. But it wasn't an unpleasant smell, and he found it kind of touching.

She came over and sat on the edge of the bed.

"Who are you, anyway?" she asked.

"My name's Jon. I play rock 'n' roll. You know that."

"No," she said, not looking at him, still embarrassed, "tell me about you. I want to know about you."

He told her about himself. About living with various relatives while his mother, the "chanteuse," worked the Holiday Inn circuit or whatever; about his aspirations to be a cartoonist, which really seemed to interest her.

"My brother used to read *Spider-Man*," she said, grinning. "I still got some of the books."

"No kidding?"

She got up and went over to the dresser. She opened a drawer and took out a three-inch stack of comics, then came back and sat on the edge of the bed and put them in Jon's lap.

They were early issues of *Spider-Man, The Fantastic Four, The Avengers*, well read but not in bad shape; not the very first issues, but within the first twenty of each. Toward the bottom of the pile he found *Amazing Fantasy* 15, which had the first Spider-Man story.

"Do you know what this is worth?" Jon said, holding it up for her to see the cover, which showed Spider-Man dragging a bad guy to justice in the sky.

"I'd never sell it."

"It's probably worth five or six hundred bucks."

She shrugged. "It was my brother's. I wouldn't sell it."

"Well, if you ever need a few bucks, these books are worth something. Particularly the *Amazing Fantasy*."

"You can have it if you want"

"I can have it?"

"Sure. My brother would want you to."

"Ron. I might not be alive tomorrow."

"Don't be stupid."

"Let me go, Ron. You can't keep me here like this."

She frowned. "I don't want to talk about it."

He let it pass. For the moment.

"Listen," she said. "Before, when we . . . you know."

"Yeah?"

"It wasn't so bad, was it?"

He smiled. "It wasn't so bad."

"You mean, you . . . liked it?"

"I liked it."

"You're not just saying that?"

"No."

"You're not just trying to get on the good side of me?"

"No."

"Are you sure?"

"Yes."

She sat there and thought about that.

Then she undid his pants again.

She stayed beside him in bed a while, curled up next to him in peasant blouse and panties, till it got dark. This time of year it got dark early, so it was probably only about five or five-thirty. He hadn't been here a full day yet, and to his knowledge, Julie hadn't been in contact with his keeper yet, either. As Ron lay sleeping beside him (or pretending to be asleep, he didn't know), he considered again the possibility of overpowering her. He could slip an arm around her neck, but unless he was prepared to kill her, that wouldn't do him any good. Not unless the key to the handcuffs was in the pocket of those jeans of hers, tossed over on the dresser. And there was no guarantee he could drag himself, by somehow dragging the bed with him, over there to find out. And the way she was softening to him, maybe keeping up the good behavior was the best way to go. But just how long he could—well, keep it up—he didn't know.

Pretty soon she rose and stretched and smiled at him, without embarrassment now, and went and put her jeans on, moving with a lack of shame and a confidence that seemed more like the old Ron, but not at all masculine.

At the doorway she stopped and turned and said, "I'm not much at cooking, except breakfast and sandwiches and that. I usually eat my meals in the kitchen at the Paddlewheel. It goes with the job. But I can stick a TV dinner in the microwave for you."

Somehow it seemed incongruous to him that she would have a microwave.

"That's fine," he said. "Anything."

She was on her way out when he called to her. "Ron?"

"What?"

"I want you to let me go."

She sighed.

"Things are going to get rougher than you know," he said. "I wasn't lying about the bank robbery. I wasn't lying about Julie trying to kill me that time. And I wasn't lying about my partner, either."

"He's a real bad-ass, this partner of yours?" There was no sarcasm at all in Ron's voice.

"That's one of the best descriptions of him I ever heard," Jon said.

She stood poised in the doorway like something in an arty photo. Then she said, "I'll think about it," and was gone.

He grinned at the door, which Ron had halfheartedly pulled shut. Only partially shut: he could hear her footsteps on the stairs very clearly.

He felt good, considering. She was going to let him go, he knew it. He'd won her over. He felt like Burt Reynolds. He'd fucked her over to his side; turned the dyke into a woman. What a man. He sat there, grinning, handcuffed.

A few minutes later, there was a banging sound downstairs: somebody at the front door. Pounding the hell out of it.

He heard the door being opened.

Ron's voice said, "What is it?"

"Things are falling apart, Ron. I need you. I need your help."

A woman's voice.

Jesus fuck. No.

Julie.

"Come in, come in," Ron said. "Is it raining out?"

The door shut.

"Drizzling," Julie said. "Cold. Icy. Maybe snow, I don't know. Listen, that kid."

"What about him?"

"I'm going to have to go away for a while."

"Yeah?"

"But I'll be back. I'll be back for you, Ron."

"You will?"

"I'm dumping that asshole Harold, and we're going to be together, you and I. But first I have to go away for a while."

"I don't understand. . . ."

"I'll have five thousand dollars in cash for you, in just a few minutes. I'm going to the club to get it, before I leave."

"Five thousand dollars? . . . For me? Why?"

"It's time."

"Time?"

"You said you could make that kid disappear for me, any time I wanted. Well, it's time. And I want it."

"What?"

"You to kill him, what do you think?"

"Kill him? I don't know . . . I don't mind sitting on him for you, but . . ."

"Ron! What's the matter with you? You said last night you'd as soon cut his throat as look at him! Since when did you care whether some goddamn man lived or died?"

There was silence.

"I want more," Ron said.

"What?"

"I want more than five thousand. I want ten."

"Well, Ron . . . we'll be together . . ."

"Maybe we'll be together and maybe we won't. I want ten."

"Okay. You got it."

"You go get the money. It'll be done when you get back."

"No. You do it now, Ron. I want it done now."

He could hear the shrug in Ron's voice. "All right."

He struggled with the cuff his wrist was in, as he heard her footsteps on the stairs, but it didn't do any good, it didn't do any goddamn fucking good, and then she was in the doorway, with a .38 in her hand.

She shut the door behind her.

"You bitch," he said, his free hand a fist.

He didn't have to swing it: his words struck her like a blow.

"Please, no," she said. Whispering. Her eyes looked wet.

She set the gun on the nightstand.

She fumbled in her front pocket The jeans she wore were tight; she had trouble finding it but then she brought it out: a small key.

She unlocked the cuff at his wrist.

"We're only one floor up," she whispered. "There's just ground under the window, not cement or anything. Hang out the window and drop."

"Ron . . ."

"I'm going to tell her you got away. I came up here and you were gone. I'm going to tell her I had you tied, and you got loose. She doesn't have to know about the cuffs."

She was undoing the cuff at his ankle.

He got up; she helped him. He was dizzy. Hard to keep balance. He started unsteadily toward his shoes.

"Never mind that," she said irritatedly, pushing him toward the window.

He grabbed her by the small of one arm. Looked at her. Touched her face.

"Get out of here," she said.

She opened the window for him, and he climbed out into the darkness, hanging by the sill, facing toward the house, and the night air felt cold, the drizzle felt good. He dropped.

The ground was hard, and one of his ankles gave, twisted. Fuck! He fell backward but was up in a second, and hobbled across the cold ground, wishing he had his goddamn shoes. This wasn't as clear a night as last night, but he could still make out the general shape of things. The old two-story farmhouse. The bare yard going back to what was apparently a plowed cornfield. Trees off to the left, which he was heading toward now.

His ankle hurt like hell, but he was so glad to be out of there and maybe, just maybe get out of Julie's grip, that the pain felt good, as good as the cold, wet air. The pain meant he was alive.

Then he was in the trees, and he could see the road: there were trees on either side of it, so it would be easy enough to head for cover if a car came. And since a car could mean Julie again, he didn't dare flag one down, so he hobbled in the road, because with his turned ankle it was better than moving through the trees and bushes and high grass. And he heard a noise behind him, back at the farmhouse. Something that could have been a shot.

He stepped up the pace, coming as close to running as a guy with a bum ankle can get; sort of a drunken jog.

Pretty soon headlights were coming up behind him, and he headed to the right, into the trees, and dropped to his stomach in the tall, wet grass; the car slowed, as if the driver had thought she (and this was certainly a she: Julie) had seen something moving in the road ahead but wasn't sure. Then moved on.

He waited what seemed forever and was possibly a couple minutes.

Then he made his way back to the road. He listened very carefully before he started his drunken jog again, listened for an idling motor, in case Julie had pulled over and cut her lights up ahead. He heard nothing, except the sound of the rain—the drizzle had already turned to rain—against the ground, the trees, the road.

He started moving again.

Should he stop at a farmhouse? There'd surely be one soon.

He didn't know if he could come up with a story that could get him safely out of this area without the cops getting into it. A guy with no shoes, looking bruised and beat-up, coming to a farmer's door for help? Assuming he didn't get shot first, what could he say?

Better to get to a town, if that didn't take forever; if luck had headed him the right direction down this road, he might end up at Gulf Port before long. A tavern there would ask no questions about his appearance, and he might even be able to bum a dime to try to call Nolan again.

But he felt sure Nolan would be on the way. He just didn't know how to connect up with him.

Up ahead there was a curve in the road. He got off to the side, so he could make a quick move off into the trees if a car came unexpectedly around it. And just as he jogged around the bend, the beams of headlights hit him like a spotlight, and he knew he'd never make the trees in time.

16

WHEN NOLAN got back to the motel room, the girl was asleep.

He sat on the bed next to her and watched her. She looked young. Very peaceful, her breasts rising, falling, with an easy rhythm. He hated to wake her. He hated to let her in on what had just happened. But he couldn't think of any way around it.

For one thing, it wasn't fair to her not to let her know what was going on here. She had to know just how rough it was getting, so she could have the option of getting out He hoped she'd decide to stay; he could use her help.

He shook her, gently.

"Oh," she said, scratching her head, her brown hair a pleasant mess. "I was dreaming."

"What about?"

"I don't remember. But it wasn't a nightmare."

"That's something, anyway."

"Right. Didn't you go to get me a Coke?"

"Yeah. I forgot it."

"That's all right. I probably shouldn't be putting any caffeine in my system anyway, not if I want to get some sleep. What's that on your shirt?"

Nolan looked down at the front of his turtleneck. "Blood," he said. "Powder burns."

"Jesus. What's going on?"

"There are some things you need to know. Sit up."

She did, and he told her about Sally and Infante breaking into his house, how they tortured Sherry, how he came in on them, killing Sally. She listened with a wide-eyed expression that tried to be interest but was mostly fear.

"Why didn't you tell me this before?" she said. No anger, just curiosity.

"I didn't want to scare you off," he said. "I thought I could use you."

She managed a smirky little smile, smoothing a hand over the bed. "I see."

"That isn't what I mean."

"I know it isn't."

"Telling you about my killing Sally makes you an accessory after the fact," he said. "That's the main reason I didn't tell you. There's always a chance, in a situation like this, that you can end up in the hands of the cops. So you were better off ignorant. I wanted your help, but I wanted to protect you, too."

"You didn't get blood on your shirt from killing Sally. That's new." She reached her finger out and touched the front of his shirt, like a kid checking if paint was dry. "That's wet."

He told her about spotting Infante's car, about the confrontation in the motel room.

She looked ill.

"This screws things up a little," he said. "I didn't intend killing Infante—not at the moment, anyway. I wanted him alive, so I could use him, to get to Jon, and handle Julie, as well. Dead, he's a problem."

"Why?"

"When Julie tries to contact him and finds him gone, she may figure I'm in town, which takes away the edge I need."

"What can we do about it?"

"Well, if Julie finds Infante's body in his room, we're as dead as he is."

She nodded. "And so is Jon."

"Right. We're better off if we get rid of the body."

"Oh, Jesus."

"There isn't much to it, really."

She shuddered. "Yeah, I know. It's the second body you've dumped today, after all."

Nolan shrugged. "It's got to be done."

"Well, give me a second."

"It's almost five. We better get this done while it's still dark."

She got out of bed and followed him out of the motel room. Neither one wore a coat, and it was cold. There was no one around; the sky was just hinting at dawn.

Nolan handed her some car keys. "These are to that little Mazda over there. It's Infante's. Back it around, right up to the edge of the sidewalk in front of the door to his room, and open the trunk."

She nodded, and went to the car, and did as she was told.

Nolan unlocked Infante's room, silenced 9 mm in hand; it was faintly possible that Julie might have showed up in the few minutes he'd been back at his own room, explaining things to the girl.

But there was no one in the room except Infante, and he was just a sprawl of leaking flesh on the carpet by the bed. Nolan took the spread off the bed and rolled Infante up in it; it was harder than it sounds. Then he went to the doorway, and the girt was standing by the open trunk.

"Nobody's around," she said, glancing from side to side, her breath visible in the air. "You need any help in there?"

"No."

"Good," she said, hugging her arms to herself, shivering, only partially from the cold.

Nolan went back and lifted the mummylike Infante into his arms, carrying him like a bride over a threshold, only Infante was going out, not in. When the girl saw the bundle in Nolan's arms, she covered her mouth.

"Shut the door," he said.

She shut the door to Infante's motel room.

"Go get the other car."

She walked down toward the Datsun. Briskly.

He laid Infante in the Mazda trunk, which was empty except for a spare tire. He had to stuff Infante in there, and bend parts of him around, as though he was fitting a piece into a puzzle, but the wrong piece. Infante would have been uncomfortable, had he been alive. Nolan shut the trunk.

The girl was there with the Datsun. It had frost on it, as did the Mazda.

He went over to where she was leaning out the rolled-down window and said, "Just follow, me," and got behind the wheel of the Mazda.

He led her down a country road lined with trees on either side. About fifteen miles out of Gulf Port, Nolan pulled the Mazda into an access inlet to a cornfield. The field was flattened and desolate looking. There were no farmhouses or barns in sight. Nolan took a handkerchief and wiped everything he'd touched: steering wheel, trunk lid, even the car keys, which he pitched out into the field. Then he left the Mazda where it was and joined the girl in the Datsun, waiting in the road nearby, motor running.

"Turn around as soon as you can," he said, "and head back to the motel."

She nodded.

When she was pulling into the stall in front of their room, Nolan said, "Now let's check Infante's room again."

"Why?"

"Don't want to leave a mess."

They got out of the car. Nolan went down and unlocked Infante's room. She followed him haltingly inside. There was a reddish-brown spot about the size of a saucer, but not as perfectly round, on the floor by the bed.

"Get a towel," Nolan said, "and get it wet and soapy."

"You want me to clean that up?"

He just looked at her.

She frowned. "Woman's work is never done," she said, and went into the bathroom.

Nolan looked under the bed. The twin to the 9 mm was there. He reached under and got it.

By this time, the girl was on her hands and knees scrubbing. She stopped for a moment, looked at the reddish-stained towel in her hands, and said, "I think I'm going to be sick."

"That's good enough," Nolan said, nodding toward the spot on the floor. "You don't want to rub it bald."

"I'll get another towel with just water and kind of rinse the area."

"Good idea."

Nolan went to the dresser and found a notepad and pen. He wrote the following on the top sheet: "Got hungry and bored. Going to Burlington for some food and a movie. Be back in a few hours." He didn't sign it, but left it out on top of the dresser. The girl looked at it.

"You think that'll hold 'em off for a while?" she asked.

"It might."

He went to the phone. He dialed the desk.

"I'm in room thirteen," he said. "I'm just getting to bed now, and I don't want to be disturbed. So don't bother sending a maid around at all today. I'll be sleeping."

"Sure," a disinterested female voice on the other end said.

"You write this down or something. I don't want to be disturbed, got it?"

"I got it," the voice, now irritated, said.

"There'll be a tip in it for you."

"Oh! Well, sure. I'm writing it down now."

"And hold my calls. I'll pick up any messages at the desk later. Just say I'm not in."

"Glad to. My name's Frances, by the way."

"Fine, Frances."

"So you'll know who to tip."

"I'll remember, Frances."

He hung up.

"Is that going to work?" the girl asked.

"It might. Take another towel and wipe off anything we touched. I never knew anybody who actually got nailed by fingerprints, except on TV. But I don't want to be the first."

He gathered Infante's clothes and the damp towels used by the girl to clean the blood up, and on the way back to their motel room, dumped it all in a trash barrel, shoving it under some other garbage.

"The sun's up," she pointed out.

"So it is," he said. "Let's get some sleep."

It was late morning when he woke and found her sitting on the edge of the bed.

"Are you okay?" he asked her.

"I don't know. I don't feel so good."

"How so?"

"My stomach hurts. I feel kind of weak."

"You're hungry."

She made a face. "Please. I dreamed I cleaned up blood with a mop and bucket all night."

"All morning. How long since you've eaten?"

"I don't know. I had lunch yesterday. I never eat a meal before a performance, so . . ."

"So you haven't eaten for a long time. You're hungry. Here." He dug in his pocket for some money and gave her two twenties.

"What's this for?"

"I want you to drive over to Burlington and find a MacDonald's or something. Someplace where you can get a breakfast to go. Eat yours there, if you like, but bring me something."

"How can you eat at a time like this?"

"The same way I can sleep, or screw."

She gave him a long, sarcastic smile, then said, "Forty bucks for breakfast is gonna buy you a truckload of Egg McMuffins, you know."

"I also want you to stop at one of those big discount stores and pick me up a shirt. Something similar to this, but without the blood and powder burns."

"Anything else?"

"Some clothesline."

"Clothesline?"

"Just enough to tie somebody up with."

She grinned. "Got ya."

"And get some toiletries. Toothbrushes, toothpaste, a shaver, shaving cream. Like that."

"Okay."

"Go."

She went—slowly, glancing back at him, afraid to go out on her own, he guessed. But she went.

He lay back on the bed and slept till she got back.

When she did, they both ate breakfast; she had waited to eat hers with him. It was MacDonald's, some pancakes, sausage, eggs. Cardboard food, but since neither of them had eaten for many hours, they wolfed it down.

Nolan took a shower, used the toothpaste. Shaved.

The shirt's a little big," he said, getting into it, "but it'll do."

"I got extra-large," she said.

"I take a large."

"Are you complaining?"

"No. I'm grateful."

"Well. You better be."

"Where's my change?"

She shook her head, and got the change out of her jeans, then handed it to him.

"It's almost two," she said. "Shouldn't we be checking on our friend Darlene?"

"Take a shower first."

"Don't be shy, Nolan. If I stink, say so."

"You'll feel better. Clean up, and we'll go."

When they did, they found the cowboy was still there; the red hot-rod pickup hadn't moved an inch.

"Shit," Nolan said, slamming the heel of his hand into the steering wheel.

"What now?"

"This is getting messy. I don't want to involve anybody else. I want the girl by herself."

"They're probably still asleep. It was after four in the morning when they got here, and they probably didn't get to sleep till five or six."

Nolan nodded. "Good point. We better just wait."

There were a few people out walking around on what was turning into a dreary, overcast Sunday afternoon. Some kids playing, none of them wearing warm enough clothing, considering the chilly weather—looking a bit ragged, in fact. A woman in a parka walking a shaggy mutt. An occasional blue-collar hippie on a motorcycle. Just enough action to make it awkward to park somewhere nearby and watch and wait.

"Back to the motel," he said.

"Jesus, I'll go stir crazy."

"It's okay. We can keep an eye out the window and see if Julie or somebody shows up knocking at Infante's door. That'd get us to Jon, too, you know."

She sighed. "I'm getting worried."

"Don't be. Wherever Jon's being held, it's likely we'll want to wait till after dark to get him anyway."

"After dark? Jesus!"

"It's dark by late afternoon this time of year. Don't worry. If he's dead, he's . . ."

"Dead. Yeah, I know. You're real comforting, Nolan."

Nolan watched a football game on TV, with the sound down; the girl sat by the window near the door, peeking through the partly drawn curtains, watching for anyone who might pull into the motel lot. It was a quiet afternoon. The only action was a few people checking out late: a couple in their twenties, dressed in an expensively casual way, walking arm in arm toward a Corvette, in an easy, worn-out fashion that bespoke a fun-filled night before; some college kids—guys—heavily hung-over, shambling out to a station wagon like the survivors of a train wreck. Otherwise nothing—no Julie. Nothing.

At five they went back to Darlene's. It was misting out; it was dark already. The red pickup was gone; but her rusting green Maverick was there. And so, presumably, was Darlene.

As soon as they got out of the car, they could hear it: a loud buzzing sound coming from within the trailer. Nolan and the girl exchanged glances, the girl shrugging, indicating that she had no idea what the sound was, either.

Nolan went up and knocked on the door, Toni at his side. He had a Bible in his right hand, supplied by the Gideons to the motel room and by the motel room to him. In his left hand, held at the moment under his jacket, was the 9 mm.

He kept knocking till the buzzing stopped.

She opened the door about halfway, looking down at Nolan (it was three steps up to the door of the trailer) with sultry, suspicious, and heavily made-up eyes. Her hair was piled high and tousled, in a calculated way, and she had on a black T-shirt with white lettering that said "STIFF RECORDS" curved over the smaller "WORLD TOUR," curved in turn over a globe, underneath which it said: "WE CAME, WE SAW, WE LEFT."

"What do you want?" she said. Her voice was flat, disinterested, her expression a bored smirk.

"We're with the Jehovah's Witnesses," Nolan said, showing her the gun in his left hand, which was hidden from view from any passersby by the Bible in his right hand.

She tried to shut the door, but Toni hopped up the steps and pushed against it with a shoulder and held it where it was, smiling at Darlene, who immediately recognized her and, after a moment, retreated into the trailer. Toni went in first and Nolan came after, shutting the door and locking it behind him.

Nolan kept his gun in hand, but tossed the Bible over on the counter in the kitchenette, which was off to the right, where a pile of unwashed dishes and beer cans and such indicated that a slob lived here. The living room was barely furnished at all: just a couch against the facing wall, a component stereo spread out on the floor over at the left, with a few big, brightly colored pillows scattered around as if the place had been ransacked. There were LP's scattered, too, and rock group posters taped to the walls. Nolan didn't recognize any of the groups; they were just so many sullen faces staring out at him. The only poster he recognized was a country performer, Willie Nelson.

In the middle of the floor, standing on newspapers, was a gray poodle; at the poodle's feet were clumps of its hair, and a clipper on a long black cord lay on the papers nearby, as well. That explained the buzzing: Darlene had been giving her poodle a haircut.

And the poodle was going nuts, barking, yapping.

Nolan walked over to it, pointed a finger at it, and it sat and shut up and looked up at him and whimpered.

"Some watchdog," Darlene said, sitting on the couch, trying to be sullen, like the faces on the posters around her. But her fear was showing. There was a pack of cigarettes on the couch next to her, and she lit up.

"You're the bitch that sings with the Nodes," Darlene said between puffs, "that much I know. Who's the guy with the gun and the Bible? And what's it all about, Alfie?"

Toni went over and grabbed a bunch of the front of Darlene's T-shirt and pushed her back against the wall. Darlene, startled, dropped her cigarette and her sullen pose; the fear in her wide, mascara-thick eyes was as apparent as the whimpering dog's.

"You're the bitch," Toni said. "The bitch who set Jon up."

Toni let go of her, and Darlene slid back down onto the couch, where she fumbled for her cigarette—and her pose—and said, "Don't know what the fuck you're talking about."

"Tell me about last night," Toni said. "Tell me about Jon and the van."

Darlene found a nasty little smile somewhere. "Will the

Jehovah's Witness get embarrassed if I said I gave the kid a blow job, and sent him on his way?"

"You're lying."

"Go fuck yourself."

Toni swung a small, sharp fist at Darlene and sent her sprawling across the couch. Darlene, on her side, felt her mouth.

"I'm bleeding," she said.

"Maybe it's just that time of the month," Toni said. She had a much more convincingly nasty smile than Darlene had mustered. Toni, taking the lead, amused and pleased Nolan.

"You fuckin' assholes," Darlene said, sitting up, trying to act mad but coming off scared. "I don't know what the fuck this is about, but you better get your asses outa here. My boyfriend's gonna be back any minute."

Toni and Nolan exchanged glances. Nolan shook his head no.

Toni said, "You're bluffing."

"Eat it."

"You set Jon up. We want to know what really happened last night. We want to know who's got him and where he is now. And you're going to tell us."

Darlene blew a smoke ring; she seemed to be getting her act together finally.

Toni motioned to Nolan, and they went over to the kitchenette area, Nolan keeping the gun pointed Darlene's way. The poodle was sitting in the midst of the papers, staring up at Nolan.

"I think I can make her talk," Toni whispered.

"You're doing fine."

"You don't mind if I handle this?"

"No. I'm enjoying myself. I'm not into knocking women around, but I don't mind watching one knock another one around."

"How about tying her up few me?"

"Fine."

Nolan got a kitchen chair and dragged it into the living room area; the poodle scooted away, running down the narrow hallway toward the bedroom to hide.

Toni pointed at the chair. "Sit in it," she told Darlene.

Darlene just sat on the couch and smoked her cigarette.

Toni grabbed her by one arm and slammed her down in the chair.

Nolan picked up the cigarette Darlene had just dropped and put it out in an ashtray on the floor near the couch. Then he took the small bundle of clothesline out of his jacket pocket and tied Darlene into the chair, and she swore at him. He ignored her; he sat down on the couch. The poodle skulked back in. It jumped up on the couch and lay next to Nolan and looked up at him pathetically; he scratched it around the collar a few times, and it rested its head on his leg.

"What's your dog's name?" he asked Darlene.

"Quiche Lorraine," she said.

"What kind of name is that?"

Toni explained. "It's from a song." She jabbed a finger at Darlene's STIFF T-shirt. "Really, Darlene, you should make up your mind. You can't be into both the B-52's *and* Willie Nelson. It just doesn't make sense."

Darlene didn't respond; she looked nervous. Being tied up didn't agree with her.

"I suppose you like to be flexible," Toni said. "It's nice to be able to come on to guys in both camps. Shitkickers and rock 'n' rollers, too. But I really think you should make up your mind, one way or another. I'm going to help you."

Toni reached down for the poodle clippers. She hit the switch, and the buzz filled the room.

"What are you doing?" Darlene shouted.

"I'm gonna give you a poodle cut," Toni said.

"No!"

"Sure. It'll be real punk. A skinhead, like in England."

"You fuckin' bitch!"

Toni grabbed a handful of the shaggy hair on top of Darlene's head and held her that way as she got behind her and started to shave at the base of her neck.

"Stop it! Stop it! I'll tell you what you want to know! Just stop it!"

Toni switched the clippers off but left the flat, wide nose of them against the base of Darlene's neck.

"What happened last night?" she asked.

"You . . . you know who Ron is?"

"That dyke you hang around with."

"Yeah. She paid me a hundred bucks to get that Jon to come out to the van."

"And?"

"She hit him over the head and put him in the back of her car."

"A hundred bucks. You helped kidnap somebody for a hundred goddamn bucks?"

Darlene managed to shrug, despite Toni's grip on her hair. "It wasn't kidnapping. She said somebody had it in for the kid and was paying her to rough him up or something. That's all I know."

Toni looked at Nolan, who was still on the couch, the poodle beside him.

Nolan said, "Can you tell us where this Ron lives?"

Darlene turned her head, which, tied in the chair as she was, was all she could turn, and looked at Nolan and said, "Sure. Why not."

Toni let loose of Darlene's hair but stood by, clippers in hand, as Darlene gave Nolan directions.

Then Nolan went to the kitchen, poodle following along after him, and found an unused dishrag in a drawer. He gagged Darlene with it. He made sure the dog had bowls full of food and water, and he and Toni left.

"That was smart," Nolan said, getting in the car, behind the wheel.

"What?"

"The poodle clippers. How d'you know that'd do the trick?"

"She's vain as hell. Didn't you notice? Sunday afternoon and she's got her makeup on, to the hilt. What for, just to give her pooch a trim? *That's* vain."

"Would you have done it?"

"Skin her? With pleasure."

They drove out of Gulf Port and down that same tree-lined road they'd been down earlier, to dump Infante. As they drove, Toni filled Nolan in on what little she knew about Ron. Nolan was doing barely forty; the mist was turning to rain, and visibility was poor. As they were coming around a curve, Nolan saw a figure, caught in the glare of his headlights, scurry off toward the side of the road, toward the trees.

"That's Jon!" he said.

He hit his brakes, threw it in park and jumped out.

"Hey, kid! It's me."

The figure stopped, turned. Across the darkness and through the rain a voice came back uncertainly: "Nolan?"

"Yeah."

Jon ran to him, grabbed him by the forearms.

"Nolan! Nolan!"

The kid was in T-shirt and jeans and socks; his face looked bruised, and his clothes were wet and dirty.

"You look like shit," Nolan said.

"You look great!"

The girl was out of the car now, and had run to Jon. She hugged him, and he hugged her back.

"Get in the car," Nolan said, "both of you."

They got in the car, Toni in back.

Quickly, Jon told Nolan what had been happening.

"You figure Julie passed you on the road here, then?" Nolan said.

"I didn't see the car, but it had to be her."

"She's probably headed for the Paddlewheel. To grab some money and run."

"I want you to drive down to that farmhouse, Nolan."

"Why?"

"I think I heard a shot. I want to check it out."

Nolan glanced at Jon.

Then he said, "Okay. There's a gun in the glove box."

Jon opened the glove compartment and took out the long-barreled .38. There was a box of shells, too, but the gun was loaded already, and Jon didn't bother with them.

Leaning forward from the back seat, her hands on the seat between Nolan and Jon, Toni said, "Let's leave. Let's get out of here. Let's go home."

Jon turned and said, "We can't. If we don't catch up with Julie now, she'll just turn up again sometime, and we don't need that shit."

"He's right," Nolan said. "We'll keep you out of it as much as possible."

"Gee, thanks," the girl said.

There was a gravel driveway leading into a larger gravel area next to the farmhouse; a barn and silo were off to the right. Nolan pulled in. There was only one car around: a vintage fifties Ford. The farmhouse was peeling paint—looked a bit run-down—but it was no hovel. There was a porch. Nolan, gun in hand, walked up the steps, and Jon followed. Toni stayed in the car, behind the wheel, windows up, doors locked.

The front door was ajar.

They went in; prowled the bottom floor, found it empty, not touching anything (though Nolan did pocket a ring of keys from a table). There was a living room, a dining room, a kitchen, a barely stocked pantry. Everything was neat, though the furniture was rather old, worn. There were a number of family portraits displayed. Unlike Darlene, Ron wasn't a slob, at least.

Upstairs, in the room Jon had been kept in, they found Ron. She was on the floor, in her peasant blouse and jeans, between the bed and the dresser. She was dead.

There was a gun in her hand, and she had a head wound. In the right temple, out the left.

"Julie never stops maneuvering, does she?" Nolan said, bending over the body.

"What?" Jon said. He looked shaken.

"Faking this as a suicide. I don't think that's a close-range wound. I think Julie shot her from the doorway. That's judging from the angle of it, the powder burns, the entry and exit wounds. But the local people may not figure it out immediately. Hard to say."

Nolan rose.

Jon knelt over the body. He touched the dead woman's cheek. He closed her eyes.

"Kid. Let's go."

"Yeah. Okay, Nolan." He rose, slowly.

"You might as well put on your shoes."

"Huh? Oh. Yeah."

His shoes were between the body and the dresser. He got them, then sat on the edge of the bed and put them on. The kid had been through a lot, Nolan thought. Maybe the girl was right; maybe they should just get the hell out. Go home.

Next to Jon on the bed was a stack of comic books.

"It never fails," Nolan laughed. "You always manage to turn up some funny-books, don't you?"

Jon looked at them. He picked them up and took them with him as they left the house. He held the comics under his shirt to protect them from the rain, as they went to the car.

Toni climbed in back and Jon got in front on the rider's side. Nolan took the wheel again. Jon handed the comics back to Toni. "Put those on the floor or something, will you?" he said.

"Okay," she said, smiling.

Both she and Nolan were amused by Jon's managing to come away from this situation with a stack of old comics.

"Any of these valuable ones?" the girl asked, kidding him.

Jon didn't seem to pick up on the kidding. "Very," he said.

"What are you going to do with 'em?" Nolan asked. "Sell 'em?"

"I wouldn't sell them. I wouldn't ever sell them." Jon opened the glove compartment and took out the box of .38 shells; he stuffed a handful of the shells in his pocket, put the box back.

"Let's go find Julie," he said.

17

SHE would have to run.

There was no other choice. Nolan was here; his breath was on her neck; and this time he wouldn't go soft and spare her, like that time at the cottage. This time he would kill her.

She knew that, and she could accept it, and she would eventually deal with it—deal with him—but now she had to run. She didn't even know where she would go. Mexico, she guessed. Money still went a long way in Mexico. And when some time had passed, she could hire somebody to do Nolan, and Jon, as well. Some other expatriate American, maybe, who could sneak back in the country and get it done.

Or something. There'd be some way out of it. There always was. Plenty of options.

But right now, running was the only option she could come up with.

The Porsche slid going around a curve, and she slowed down; the blacktop was slick with rain. *Don't panic now,* she told herself. But the rain and the darkness, crowding her on the narrow blacktop that led to the Paddlewheel, seemed to be on Nolan's side.

She had been so sure she was on top of this Nolan situation, it made her smug; so sure she was in control of things, it made her complacent. When she thought about how she'd spent the morning and afternoon, she could kick herself: sleeping till noon, sitting in Harold's study with a gin and tonic, explaining to him her plans for Nolan, playing down the role of that slug Infante. (In the version she told Harold, Infante would be on hand only as protection, in case Nolan didn't uphold his end of the swap she would propose.)

Still, Harold had seemed morose; it was almost as if he had seen through what she told him, that he knew she really intended having Nolan and Jon killed. He had sat in his study all afternoon, listening to an old Beatles album, *Revolver,* he seemed to enjoy feeling sorry for himself, and the world, his lips moving to the lyrics of "Eleanor Rigby," for Christ's sake. What a jerk. She didn't know why she'd put up with him for so long.

On the other hand, there was a part of her that liked him and his self-pitying ways. He wasn't a stupid man—he certainly came in handy at the club, doing the books, handling the staff— and she liked having a big, reasonably competent man around, who depended on her, whom she could mother into submission. She'd always had a knack for finding men who needed a mother in a woman, and having all but raised most of her brothers and sisters, she was used to playing mother—though it occasionally struck her as ironic that she had never spent enough time with her own kid to really qualify in that department.

So as Harold sat in his study, listening to old Beatle records, she felt a weird mixture of contempt and affection for him—a man his age, sitting there feeling sorry for himself, losing himself in memories of high school. It was fucking pathetic. . . .

Around three she had called the motel to talk to Infante. She needed to go have a talk with him, alone, without Harold around, to fill Infante in on what her plans really were where Nolan and Jon were concerned. But the woman on the desk said Infante was out. It struck Julie as strange, but not suspicious, particularly, at least not at first. When she called back around quarter to five and got the same response from the desk clerk, she put aside her gin and tonic and her book on refinishing antiques and grabbed her coat. She stuck her little pearl-handled automatic in her purse and told Harold she would be back soon.

She knocked on Infante's motel room door and got no answer.

The woman at the desk, a thin, plain woman about forty, doing the crossword puzzle in the Sunday paper, shrugged without looking up, saying all she knew was the night clerk had left a note saying the man in room 13 had requested not to be disturbed, and that if anyone called, to say he was out. Julie asked to speak to the night clerk, and was told she wouldn't be on duty till midnight. When Julie insisted, the woman gave her the night clerk's phone number, and she called her from a booth outside the motel.

"That's right," a sleepy female voice said. "He wasn't *really* going anyplace. Just wanted some sleep. Like I do. Do you mind?"

"So he wasn't going out?"

"I was supposed to say he was out and take messages."

"I see. Tell me. Did anybody check in last night after two?"

"Everybody checked in last night after two. Couples, mostly. Get the idea?"

"Any singles? A man maybe?"

"No single men. There was this girl."

"Girl?"

"Pretty brown-haired girl. Not real big."

"What was she wearing?"

"I don't know. T-shirt and jeans, I guess."

"Do you remember anything specific? There's money in it if you do."

"Well. The T-shirt had the name of a rock group on it."

"Oh?"

"Not some big group, like Kiss or something. A band from around here, whose name I recognized."

"What was it?"

"The Nodes. Ever hear of 'em?"

Julie went back to the check-in desk and, for twenty bucks, the clerk tore herself away from her crossword long enough to give her the key to room 13. There Julie found a note, presumably from Infante, saying he'd gone out for a bite to eat and a movie. She looked around the room carefully. She noticed two things: there were no towels in the bathroom, and there was a damp spot on the floor near the bed.

She was driving back to the house, down the tree-lined country lane along which Ron also lived, when she noticed a car, apparently abandoned, pulled into one of the access inroads to a cornfield. She must have passed it before, on her way to the motel, but hadn't noticed it. Now she did: a Mazda. Infante's car.

She stopped and got out and had a look, not touching

anything. It was empty; the keys weren't in the dash. But she had a feeling the trunk wasn't empty.

She got back in her Porsche.

Somehow that kid Jon had gotten a message to Nolan. Maybe there was another phone at the Barn, one she hadn't known about. Maybe Jon had used Bob Hale's private phone. That was probably it. Damn! Whatever the case, the kid had obviously got to Nolan, because Nolan was here already; Infante was dead, most likely; and she was shit out of luck.

She pulled into the driveway of her house and stood poised in front of the pillared structure like the heroine on the cover of a gothic paperback. There was no sign of Nolan yet. The only other car around was Harold's Pontiac Phoenix, in the garage, where it was supposed to be. She went in the back way, through the kitchen, gun in hand. But there was nobody in the house except Harold, still sitting in the study, listening to Beatle records: "All the lonely people . . ."

"What are you sneaking around for?" he asked, turning down the stereo, eyeing the little automatic in her hand.

"He's here," she said, putting the gun back in her purse. "Nolan's here."

"Jesus Christ."

She went upstairs and started packing a bag. He was at her side as she did.

"I'll get in touch with you," she said. "It may be a few months."

"I'm not going with you?"

"No. The Paddlewheel is too good a thing to throw away. We're going to try to hold onto it. You're going to hold onto it for me."

"Where will you be?"

"I don't know yet. And when I do know, I won't tell you. If you don't know, you can't tell anybody."

That hurt him. "*Tell* anybody? What . . ."

"Look. Nolan will show up, and when he does, the less you know, the better, because you're probably going to have to take some heat from him. But he's not going to kill you or anything."

"Well, that's nice to know."

"Harold. Just play dumb. You can handle it."

"Your confidence in me is overwhelming."

The bag was packed.

She put a hand on his shoulder. "You'll come through for me. You always have."

He smiled wearily; he nodded.

"Now," she said, carrying the bag out of the room, heading down the stairs, Harold trailing after, "you go to the Paddlewheel. I'm going to need that getaway money."

"The hundred thousand?" Harold said.

"Yes. I can live a long time on that."

She was at the front door. He grabbed her arm. Softly.

"Don't leave me," he said.

"Harold," she said, pulling away, "I'm not going to leave you. I'm just getting my butt out of here before it gets shot off. I'll be back. I like my life here. I'm not giving it up easily." She kissed him on the mouth, hastily, and said, "I'll meet you at the Paddlewheel in twenty minutes, half an hour."

"Where are you going?"

"To Ron's."

He grabbed her arm again, hard this time. "Why?"

"To tell her to let that kid go, that's why. That should cool Nolan off a little."

He let go. Licked his lips nervously. "Oh," he said.

"See you at the club."

The person who answered the door at the farmhouse seemed to be Ron, but Julie couldn't be sure. It was a not unattractive woman with makeup on and a peasant blouse and jeans; also a choking cloud of perfume. Yet this apparently *was* Ron.

And Ron's attitude didn't seem to have changed: she was more than willing to kill the kid, for a price.

Only when she went upstairs to do it, she was gone too long, and Julie followed up after her.

Ron was alone in the room. She was busy undoing handcuffs that were hanging on the bedposts. Her gun, a long-barreled revolver, was on the nightstand. The window was open; cold air was coming in.

Ron seemed startled when she noticed Julie in the doorway.

"Little bastard got away," she explained.

"I see," Julie said.

"I don't know how he got out of these things," she said, taking the handcuffs over toward the dresser, turning to lay them on top of it, facing a mirror all but obscured by taped-on pinups of Elvis Presley and others.

"Neither do I," Julie said, and picked up the revolver and shot Ron through the head.

She put the gun in Ron's hand; with some luck, it would pass for suicide. Ron would just be that sullen lesbian who finally ended it all.

And now Julie was pulling her Porsche into the unlit Paddlewheel lot. Harold was already there; his Phoenix was over by the front door. They were closed Sundays, so there was no problem with staff or customers being around. There was no sign of Nolan, though that didn't mean anything. She got the little automatic out of her purse. Her suitcase was in the trunk; she was ready to go. All she needed was her money, and no Nolan.

She walked to the front door and unlocked it, glad Harold hadn't left it open. At least he was thinking. She went in, locking the door behind her. Harold had turned on a few lights, just enough to for her to navigate, and to get a look at some of what she was leaving behind.

She walked through the entryway, past the hat check area and the rest rooms, and stood for a moment at the top of the few steps that led down into the dining room. It was a big room, full of tables with red cloths and candles; a mural of a paddlewheel boat extended along the wall at left; and a huge picture window stood across a room from her—with a magnificent river view— though with this rainy, murky night you couldn't see much of it now. The room otherwise had been left the natural (though sandblasted) brick of the warehouse it had been; the kitchen was off to the left.

She was proud of what she had accomplished here. When she took over a year ago, the restaurant had barely been breaking even, though of course the casino downstairs (which then as now was open on Friday and Saturday nights only) had been doing a good business. If she hadn't seen the potential of the place, that time Harold brought her here to eat when she was staying with him after the Port City robbery, she wouldn't be in this mess, she supposed; she wouldn't have settled so dangerously close to where she lived before. But she'd seen the potential, all right. And found from Harold that the original owner—a guy named Tree, with mob connections—had moved to Des Moines to open a similar place, leaving this one to be run, rather incompetently it seemed, by hired hands. So she'd approached Tree and his Family friends with an offer to buy controlling interest in the place, and she had really made a go of it. She was, it turned out, a natural businesswoman.

And that was the surprise, really; all those years she was working in a beauty shop, waiting for some rich fucker to come along and make her life easy, it never occurred to her that she might want to work, that a life of luxury was a bore and the challenge of making money was almost as good as spending it.

Oh, she liked eating well and living well; she liked her fancy house and her antiques.

But what she really liked was her role as owner of the Paddlewheel; she liked that as much as the money that came with it. And she wasn't going to give it up. She'd be back. She would be back.

She headed down the stairs, a stairway enclosed only from the railing down, and crossed the small casino room, with its card tables and several craps tables and one roulette wheel, and slots off to either side, and walked toward the bar, off to the right of which was Harold's cubbyhole office.

He was sitting behind his desk; the money was on top of it. Stacks of money packets, still in their bank wrappers.

"Put that in something," she said.

His eyes looked sad, like a basset hound with glasses. "I don't have anything."

"There's a paper sack lining your wastebasket. Use that."

He nodded, emptied his wastebasket on the floor, removed the sack, and started filling it with the packets of money; he looked like a bag boy at a supermarket.

"What about Ron?" he asked.

"Dead," she said.

He flinched, but he kept dropping packets in the sack. "What happened?"

"The kid got away. I don't know how he managed it. He killed her before he left. Put the gun in her hand to try to make it look like suicide."

"My God. So they're both loose?"

"I wouldn't sweat the kid. He's probably wandering around a cornfield somewhere. It's Nolan who's the threat. Okay, that's good. Hand it here."

He handed her the sack. The desk was between them.

"I have to go," she said.

"I'll miss you," he said.

"I'll miss you, too," she said. Meaning it.

"You *will* be back?"

"I'll be back," she snapped. "I'm no idiot. This is a good gig."

"Yes. Right."

She leaned across the desk and gave him a big, long kiss on the mouth. She smiled at him. She really did hope he could live through whatever Nolan might do to him. "I'll be back before you know it, lover."

He mustered a pathetic, self-pitying smile. "Do that," he said.

"Are you going to stay here for a while?"

"Yes. I'm going to work on the books."

"He's liable to show up any time. Nolan, I mean."

"Okay."

"You have a gun?"

"No."

"Good I don't want you to. I don't want you getting into it with him. You have to be just some poor innocent sucker I involved in this, as far as he's concerned, understand?"

He nodded.

"Okay, then. Take care of yourself."

"You too."

He was still standing behind the desk when she left him.

Approaching the stairs, she heard the sound of footsteps above. Faint, but definitely footsteps. She ducked around the side of the stairs, knelt so that the enclosed part of the stairway hid her. She put her sack of money down. She still had the automatic in her hand.

Somebody was coming down the stairs.

It seemed like a year before the figure emerged at the bottom. He'd been looking around the room, slowly, as he came down, apparently.

It was Nolan, of course.

She wished she had a bigger gun, but the automatic would have to do. She grabbed it by its short barrel and clubbed him on the back of the head with the butt, and he went down.

18

NOLAN EASED into the Paddlewheel lot. Over to the left a Porsche was parked; a Pontiac was parked up near the front door. No one in either car, apparently. Nolan put the Datsun in park, leaving the motor on, the car turned sideways so that it blocked the exit of the lot. The rain wasn't coming down hard, but it was insistent, pattering the roof of the car as if the sky was slightly leaky.

"I'm going in," Nolan said.

"I'm going with you," Jon said.

"No."

"Nolan . . ."

"I know. You're pissed. You been put through the mill, and you're pissed. That's just what I need right now: you—acting like a psychopathic nut."

Jon didn't say anything; he affected a sort of scowl; it came off more like a pout.

It was deceptively peaceful, sitting in this car in the rain, rain shadows from the streaky windshield throwing abstract patterns on their faces. Rain dancing on the car roof. Contemplative. And underneath it, a current of something not at all peaceful.

Leaning up from the back seat, the girl said, "How do you even know they're in there? Maybe they took some other car and left these behind."

"You're right," Nolan said. "They could even be outside there in the bushes, waiting for us to get out of the car."

"Oh, nice thought," the girl said, her sarcasm not quite masking her fear.

"Going in after them is probably a bad idea in the first place," Nolan said. "The smart thing might be to wait outside for them. If they're in there, they'll have to come out sooner or later."

"Then why not wait?" the girl asked.

"Impatience," Nolan said, shrugging. "Also, as you say, we don't know for a fact they're in there. You know what's on the other side of that building? The river. Which means they may have hopped in a boat and gone to Iowa already."

"Or," Jon said, "they might be inside, getting that money together I heard her and Ron talking about, and then go for a boat ride."

Nolan nodded. "Except I think Julie'll go and leave that big boyfriend of hers behind for me to play with."

"Yeah," Jon said. "You're probably right."

"I think she's in there," Nolan said. "This has all been breaking too fast for her to be anywhere else."

"Won't that place be locked up?" the girl asked. In the rain, with its sign off, the building across the graveled lot looked much more like a warehouse than a restaurant.

Nolan reached in his pocket for the ring of keys. "I got these at that farmhouse," he said. "Jon said that Ron was a night watchman of sorts at the Paddlewheel. With any luck at all, these'll get me in."

"You want this?" Jon asked, holding the long-barreled .38 out to Nolan in his palm, like an offering.

"You hold onto that," Nolan said, picking up the 9 mm from the seat between him and Jon. "I've got over half a clip left in this, and a spare, so if I have to exchange a few rounds with 'em, I can."

"Jesus," the girl said.

"But if you hear gunfire, you'll know it's them, not me," Nolan went on, pointing to the silencer attached to the automatic. "So you may have to come in and back me up."

"Where does that leave me?" the girl said.

Nolan turned and looked at her. "Just get behind the wheel and stay with this car blocking the way as long as you can. If Julie and her boyfriend come piling out of there with guns in their hands, before us, you got my permission to haul ass out."

"Why don't we just leave?" the girl said. "Why don't we just go home? This is crazy."

"I'm sorry you're involved in this," Nolan said. "But I told you I could drop you at a bar or motel or something, and you said no. So just keep your eyes open, and pitch in if you're needed."

Nolan got out of the car. So did Jon. He came around to Nolan's side. Nolan was looking around, looking for movement; he hadn't been kidding when he'd told Toni somebody might be waiting in the bushes. The rain was coming down harder now — not a downpour, but they were getting wet standing there.

"You're going to have to do it this time, Nolan."

"Kill her, you mean? Yeah, I know. I'm not nuts about shooting a woman, even if it is Julie. But that bitch is the fucking plague."

"It has to be done. You're sure you don't want me with you?"

Nolan smiled, put a hand on the kid's damp shoulder. "You're my insurance policy. Come in if you hear shooting. Otherwise, stick with the girl. Let's get her out of this alive, what do you say?"

"I'm for that," Jon said, smiling.

"I'm going in a side door," Nolan said, pointing off to the left of the brick building. "Bob Hale gave me a rough layout of the place. The kitchen should be over there. I'll leave the door open, in case you have to follow me in."

"Right."

"See you in a few minutes, kid."

"See you."

Nolan headed across the gravel at a slow jog. The gravel extended around the side of the building, where he found two doors, the first having no window, the second, down a ways, having a window with a grillwork through which he could make out what seemed to be the kitchen.

He started trying the keys on the ring; the fifth one opened the door. The Yale lock made a click that sounded loud as a gunshot to him, but he went on in, not hesitating, standing just inside for a while, leaving the door ajar, listening to see if his coming in had attracted anybody's attention. He stood there a good three minutes and heard nothing.

He was in a kitchen, all right, a big room with natural brick walls, but appointed white; it seemed spotless, too, though there wasn't much light in here to tell, just a small fixture on the wall inside the door, left permanently on, apparently. He moved past a row of stoves and pushed open a door that led into a small service area; he managed to avoid bumping into the trays on stands lining the wall, full of silverware, condiments, and the like. At the next door he listened for another minute or so, heard nothing, then pushed it open and went on into the big dining room.

There were some lights on. Just enough to get around without stumbling into things. And enough to get a look at the place, and see what it was that Julie was trying to hold onto. It was a nice layout, reminding him just a little of the Pier. The steamboat mural and the river view made this dining room a natural; with decent food, you couldn't fail here.

He walked as softly as he could, but the floor wasn't carpeted; it was a waxed wood floor that wanted to echo your footsteps. He knew there were two other levels, but Hale had told him he thought Julie's office was upstairs, and her boyfriend's down. Since they'd be together, most likely, it seemed to Nolan a toss-up as to which office they'd be in. Hers seemed slightly more likely, so he decided to check the downstairs first and get it out of the way.

He went down the stairs slowly, looking the casino room over—nothing elaborate, a small setup designed probably for the weekend trade. And he listened. Across the room, down by the bar, to the right, a door was partially open; lights were on within.

This was it, then; soon it would be over.

He stepped off the last step and stood there, looking toward that partially opened door, and something slammed into the back of his head.

He went down, not out, but while he didn't lose consciousness, exactly, he wasn't exactly on top of things, either.

By the time he knew what was what, he was sitting up, rubbing the back of his head, and Julie was pointing two guns at him, one of them his. Or Sally's, actually: the silenced 9 mm. The other gun was a little .22 automatic that looked like a toy, the sort of toy the PTA would like banned.

She was smiling, and he'd never seen anything quite like it— nothing as beautiful, or as ugly, as that smile.

She was standing over him, just a few paces away, wearing designer jeans and a suede coat, open in front to reveal a pale green blouse and the shelf of her breasts. There was a purse tucked under one arm, and a paper sack at her feet; the top where the sack had been twisted shut had loosened up, and packets of money were peeking out

She was stunning: the brown hair frosted blonde; perfect features, with subtle makeup; tits he wanted to touch, even as he sat there knowing she would kill him, any time now.

Well, he thought. *Might as well play out the hand . . .*

"Where's Jon?" he demanded.

She shrugged. "He got away from me. He's wandering around the countryside, as far as I know."

"I don't believe you."

"I don't care."

"Listen. I don't give a damn about you, or the money you took that was partly mine. I just want that kid back." He started to get up.

"Stay put," she said. Pointing the 9 mm at his head.

From the doorway down by the bar, the boyfriend came out and walked across the empty casino room, moving slowly between the various tables; a big, sandy-haired man with glasses, and a face that was the saddest thing Nolan ever saw.

Julie turned and smiled at him as he came up beside her; she handed him the toylike .22, keeping the silenced automatic for herself.

"Harold," she said, "I don't think I'm going to be leaving after all."

"You're going to kill him?"

"I'm going to take him up to the kitchen," she said. "It'll be easier to clean up afterwards."

"What about the boy?"

"Jon? He'll show up, probably. Eventually. I'm not worried about him. I'll handle it when the time comes." She looked toward Nolan with respect in her smile. "This is the guy to worry about. But not for much longer."

Nolan said, "Isn't it a little messy, a little dangerous, shooting me on your own property? In your restaurant? Why not take me out in the boonies somewhere?"

"You'd do anything to buy a little time, wouldn't you, Nolan?" she said.

"You killed Ron, didn't you?" Harold said to her.

"What?" Julie said, not following him.

Nolan picked up on it. "That's right. I just came from there, that farmhouse. She wanted Ron to kill the kid, but Ron wouldn't do it let him go instead. Then your princess here shot Ron in the head and faked it up like suicide."

She looked at Nolan, just a little amazed.

"Get up," she told him. "We're going to the kitchen."

Nolan rose. "She's the plague, Harold. Haven't you figured that out yet? Everything she touches turns to dead."

She turned to Harold and smiled like a madonna. "You stay down here. I can take care of this myself."

Harold said, "I love you, Julie."

"I know you do, Harold."

He shot her in the right eye.

It knocked her back, left her sprawled across the bottom few steps of the staircase, a tear of blood tracing her cheek under where her eye had been. She looked at Harold out of the remaining one, or seemed to, anyway.

Nolan let out some air. Cautiously, he reached down and picked up the 9 mm, which Julie dropped when she died.

"Thanks," Nolan said.

"Don't mention it" the big man said, and turned the toy .22 on himself and looked down the barrel and watched death come out.

19

CRACKING sounds, first one, then another, seconds later; gunshots, Jon was sure of it. Faint, but gunshots.

Despite his turned ankle, he ran, .38 in hand, Toni calling out behind him, telling him to be careful. He found the door to the kitchen open and almost ran into Nolan, coming through the service area beyond the kitchen.

"Nolan! Are you all right?"

"I'm fine."

Nolan had a paper bag in one hand.

"What's that?" Jon asked.

"A sack full of money."

"No kidding? How much?"

"I don't know. Want to sit down and count it?"

"Maybe we ought to get out of here."

"Yeah."

Going through the kitchen, Jon said, "What happened?"

Nolan told him quickly; he was finishing his story by the time they reached the Datsun in the lot. When they got in, Nolan taking the wheel, Toni climbing in back again, Jon started telling her the story and was finished by the time they were going over the old rumbling metal bridge into Burlington.

"Killed himself?" she said, not quite believing it.

"That's right," Jon said. "Poor bastard killed himself."

"No, he didn't," Nolan said.

Jon looked at Nolan.

So did Toni.

"Beauty killed the beast," Nolan said.

Nolan handed the guy in the toll booth the round-trip token and drove on.

About the Author

Max Allan Collins, who created the graphic novel on which the Oscar-winning film *Road to Perdition* was based, has been writing hard-boiled mysteries since his college days in the Writers Workshop at the University of Iowa. Besides the books about Nolan, the criminal who just wants his piece of the American dream, and killer-for-hire Quarry, he has written a popular series of historical mysteries featuring Nate Heller and many, many other novels. At last count, Collins's books and short stories have been nominated for fifteen Shamus awards by the Private Eye Writers of America, winning for two Heller novels, *True Detective* and *Stolen Away*. He lives in Muscatine, Iowa with his wife, Barbara Collins, with whom he has collaborated on several novels and numerous short stories. The photo above shows Max in 1971, when he was first writing about Nolan and Quarry.

Hard-boiled heists by Max Allan Collins

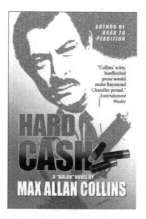

FLY PAPER
Max Allan Collins
162 pages $13.95
ISBN: 978-1-935797-22-7
"Collins is a master."
Publishers Weekly

HARD CASH
Max Allan Collins
150 pages $13.95
ISBN: 978-1-935797-23-4
"Witty, hardboiled prose."
Entertainment Weekly

HUSH MONEY
Max Allan Collins
180 pages $13.95
ISBN: 978-1-935797-24-1
"A damned fine writer!"
Armchair Detective

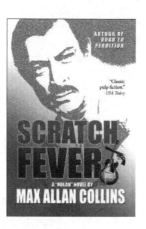

MOURN THE LIVING
Max Allan Collins
172 pages $13.95
ISBN: 978-1-935797-25-8
"Never misses a beat!"
Booklist

SCRATCH FEVER
Max Allan Collins
164 pages $13.95
ISBN: 978-1-935797-26-5
"Classic pulp fiction."
USA Today

SPREE
Max Allan Collins
212 pages $14.95
ISBN: 978-1-935797-27-2
"An exceptional storyteller!"
San Diego Union

Killer for hire: 5 classics by Max Allan Collins

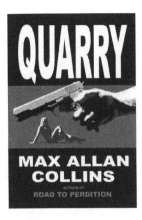

QUARRY
Max Allan Collins
234 pages $14.95
ISBN: 978-1-935797-01-2
"Packed with sexuality."
USA Today

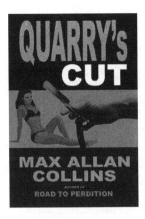

QUARRY'S CUT
Max Allan Collins
182 pages $13.95
ISBN: 978-1-935797-04-3
"Classic pulp fiction."
USA Today

QUARRY'S DEAL
Max Allan Collins
190 pages $13.95
ISBN: 978-1-935797-03-6
"Violent and volatile."
USA Today

QUARRY'S LIST
Max Allan Collins
164 pages $13.95
ISBN: 978-1-935797-02-9
"Never misses a beat!"
Booklist

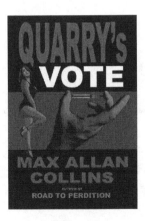

QUARRY'S VOTE
Max Allan Collins
214 pages $14.95
ISBN: 978-1-935797-05-0
*Quarry versus a
political cult.*

*Nobody's
harder-boiled
than Quarry.*

*Each title with
a new Afterword
by the Author.*

New York private eye Miles Jacoby

EYE IN THE RING
Robert J. Randisi
July 2012 $12.95
ISBN: 978-1-935797-40-1
"He's one of the best."
Michael Connelly

BEATEN TO A PULP
Robert J. Randisi
July 2012 $12.95
ISBN: 978-1-935797-41-8
"A masterful writer."
James W. Hall

HARD LOOK
Robert J. Randisi
July 2012 $12.95
ISBN: 978-1-935797-42-5
"Stripped for speed."
Loren D. Estleman

FULL CONTACT
Robert J. Randisi
July 2012 $12.95
ISBN: 978-1-935797-43-3
"Shades of James M. Cain."
Harlan Ellison

STAND-UP
Robert J. Randisi
July 2012 $12.95
ISBN: 978-1-935797-44-9
"Last of the pulp writers."
Booklist

SEPARATE CASES
Robert J. Randisi
July 2012 $12.95
ISBN: 978-1-935797-45-6
"Best of the Jacoby books."
Jeremiah Healy

Made in the USA
Middletown, DE
10 August 2015